NEWTON FREE LIBRARY

~~330 HG~~

NEWTON, MA 02459

3/16

W9-BFN-330

Starring

WITHDRAWN

Eliza

Abby Richmond

Other Books by Abby Richmond

Very Berry

Copyright © 2011 Abby Richmond. All rights reserved.

To all my friends and family.
You inspire me every day!

Prologue

I refused to move. My parents absolutely couldn't make me. Hello? I was *not* going to move. Not if I could help it.

My name is Eliza Hawthorne and I am eleven and three-quarters years old. I like friendship bracelets, being a playwright, cushy beanbag chairs, gardening, going on nature walks, and s'mores. I currently live in San Francisco, in a stylish apartment where I can look out the big windows and see the fog rolling in over the Golden Gate Bridge. It is amazing.

Now, normally I am an agreeable person, but I couldn't agree to this idea. I didn't like it one bit. Why move? I was happy here. Why were my parents going crazy?

Why were they making me move?

"What?" Sydney asked, dropping her box of crayons.

"Wow!" Poppy squealed.

But unlike me, they actually looked excited about the whole we're-moving-to-a-place-that-is-across-the-entire-country idea. Poppy did a slightly messy cartwheel, while Sydney twirled around the room, humming under her breath. Thankfully, I knew they wouldn't be so thrilled on the plane. Probably.

Four-year-old twin sisters can be such a pain sometimes.

"No! Are you serious? But we've lived here forever," I moaned. "I won't go!"

"But, Eliza, you're going to love it," Dad said. "You lived there when you were little, only in a different town, remember?"

"I lived there up until I was five! I don't even remember it! You just *can't* make me leave San Francisco!" Oh my gosh, this was not happening!

"Come on, Eliza, it's beautiful! Wilderness surrounding you. You know you love that," my mom coaxed.

"There are no redwood trees in the Berkshires," I said.

"That's true," my dad admitted, defeated.

"But there's nature everywhere," Mom said.

"You already said that!" I snapped. I walked stiffly to my room, slamming the door. I collapsed onto my purple fuzzy beanbag. I told myself not to cry. I'm not a crybaby.

To distract myself, I decided I would make a friendship bracelet for each of my closest friends at the Golden Gate Bridge School. I picked out three colors for each person.

Cross over, make a knot. Repeat. Cross over,

make a knot. Repeat. Cross over, make a knot. Repeat. Move on to the next color.

I'm moving, too, I thought sadly. These were my farewell presents. Tears slipped down my cheeks.

So much for not crying.

● ●

It was lunchtime at the Golden Gate Bridge School, which normally should have been a buzzing time when I sat with my friends Jordi, Karynn, and Angela. But today we sat in dead silence. I hate silence.

"Well, I made friendship bracelets for all of you…um…so we can remember the good times that we had…" I started lamely.

Jordi glared at me, her eyes hurt and unfriendly. Karynn raised her eyebrows. Angela smiled at me, but half-heartedly. I bit my lip. I felt so stupid!

"Here," I tossed the first one at Jordi. Neon green, hot pink, and white stripes. She snatched hers and didn't say thank you. Neither did Karynn. Angela was the only one who took hers politely. She put it in her pocket.

"Guys, I don't want to move," I explained. I wanted them to say that they knew, they would write letters, they would keep in touch. Jordi, my best friend. *She* would.

But somehow, deep inside, I knew she wouldn't. Because sometimes, she could be pretty mean to others when she was upset.

And Jordi narrowed her eyes at me. "You're moving to the BERKSHIRES, Eliza. What a dumb place to move to. And we all know that you actually *do* want to move away, because you think you're too good for us."

The unkindness and unfairness of this felt as though Jordi had slapped me on my face.

Or on my heart.

And when I got up and ran from the table, out of the corner of my eye, I saw Jordi throw her bracelet deep down into the bottom of her backpack.

Chapter One

I opened my eyes to find my twin sisters hovering over my face.

"Wake up, wake up!" Poppy and Sydney said. "We're almost here!"

I groaned and stretched. The pilot was blabbering over the loudspeaker about what temperature and time it was in the Berkshires, and how long it took us to get here. I massaged my neck. It hurt. I felt extremely cramped. I shut my eyes again as if it were all just a dream.

"Eliza, we're in Massachusetts!" Mom exclaimed. Dad squeezed my hand.

"We're in Mathachuset, we're in Mathachuset!"

"Mass-a-chu-setts," Dad corrected. "Pop, can you fold up the trays? We're going to land soon."

But Poppy couldn't because she had started crying. So had Sydney. Their ears hurt. My ears hurt listening to them. Unfortunately, about five more little kids started wailing too. I looked at my parents accusingly.

"Hey, it isn't my fault," Dad replied.

"We'll be off this plane soon," Mom said.

Even though I was really annoyed, I helped comfort my sisters. Although they got on my nerves, I felt bad for them. I remembered when I was four and my ears would kill when we landed in a plane. I braided Sydney's blond locks and played a hand game with Poppy. They both quieted down.

"Thank you for flying with our airlines," an automated voice said on the loudspeaker after we landed. "We hope you have a nice trip."

Yeah, I thought. *Only ours isn't a trip. We're staying here.*

As we walked into the quiet airport, I felt both sadness and a thrill of excitement. Back in San Francisco, Jordi and Karynn didn't even care that I was gone. It was silly of me to think they would understand. I suddenly remembered what they had done when Izzi Gardner left. I realized with a pang that probably only Angela, the kindest girl in our class, but not as close to me as Jordi, would write to me. But the Berkshires held a whole new opportunity for me. I would make new friends, go to a new school, and live in a scenic place. Sure, San Francisco was scenic with all the redwood trees, but the nature was kind of far away from the apartment. Whereas here I'd practically be living in the wilderness, like Mom kept telling us. But I would miss San Fran a ton.

When I snapped out of my little daydream, I

saw Sydney looking up at me curiously. "Whatcha doing?" she asked.

"Nothing," I told her, a bit wistfully.

Sydney slipped her little hand into mine and smiled. Poppy caught sight of that and hurried over to me. That girl loves attention.

When Mom and Dad left to go pick up the luggage, they left me in charge.

"E-wiza," Poppy said, "are you gonna miss San Francisco?"

"Yeah, I will," I said. "But the Berkshires are going to be great." I tried to muster a lot of enthusiasm, for the twins' sake.

"You promise?" Sydney asked. She gripped my hand tightly. She looked up at me, her Hawthorne-trademark blue eyes worried. We all had those eyes, except for Poppy, who had brown eyes.

"Yes," I said seriously.

Mom and Dad hurried through the crowd, carrying most of our belongings (in suitcases, of course!). All our other stuff would be shipped from California. Mom thrust our jackets at us.

"Put them on. It's cold in the Berkshires at night," she said, pulling on her blue coat. I put on my own tan corduroy jacket. Dad helped Sydney and Poppy zip theirs up.

We left the airport and caught a taxi. While we were in the taxi, my parents reminded us that we were moving to a town in the Berkshires called Sparrow.

"Sparrow is such an amazing place," my mom said. "It has neighborhoods that are like the neighborhoods you write about in your plays, Eliza, with pretty houses and beautiful views."

"The school you're going to go to in the fall is called Sparrow Middle School. It's highly recommended. It's supposed to be great, even though it's small," Dad continued.

I looked over at the twins. They were already asleep.

"You know, there's a girl your age on the block…what's her name again?"

I couldn't help it – I fell asleep.

● ●

I woke up on a strange air mattress, hearing a strange noise. The doorbell!

I quickly jumped off the mattress I was laying on top on. I looked around the room, thinking I was in San Francisco. Nope. I was in a plain, white room. There was no carpeting on the floor. But I didn't have time to look around right now. Mom and Dad weren't awake yet, so I hurried to get dressed. I peeked for any boxes that held my clothing. But I guessed Dad hadn't brought the boxes upstairs yet. At least I was still actually wearing my clothes from yesterday. Scowling, I slowly found my way to the front door. I didn't stop to check out what everything looked like. I opened the door and poked my head out. The girl was just about to turn around and leave, I'd taken so long.

"Hey!" I yelled. *Great,* I thought. *Mom and Dad are definitely awake now.*

"Hi!" The girl rushed back to the door. She was holding a plate covered in tinfoil in her arms. Whatever it was, it smelled good. She looked over at me with concern. I knew I looked like a mess. "Oh no, is this a bad time?"

I winced. "It's fine." I rubbed at my eyes sleepily. The girl was a little smaller than me, with blond hair worn in a headband. She had ice blue eyes, like me, framed in green glasses. She wore a sweatshirt with SPARROW stitched onto the side, and jeans. Her sneakers had seen better days. They were scuffed up but the girl didn't seem to care.

The Sneaker Girl said, "My name is Olympia Barnes. But call me Ollie. Olympia is much too long. Anyway, I live down the block. Welcome to Sparrow. My mom made these and told me to give them to you. She says, quote un-quote, that 'the morning you've moved in is the hardest of 'em all, so there is absolutely no time to make your own breakfast.' In case you were wondering, they're blueberry pancakes."

So this was the kid who lived on the block that Mom and Dad were jabbering about in the taxi!

"Thanks," I mumbled. "My name is Eliza Hawthorne." The stairs creaked and the next thing I, Eliza Hawthorne, knew, my parents were right beside me.

"Hello," Mom said warmly. "You must be Olympia."

Ollie nodded. "Yes, ma'am. Only I prefer Ollie."

"Ollie brought pancakes for our breakfast," I said.

"How kind of you," my dad said. He patted his stomach. "They smell good! Thanks."

Ollie laughed. "You're welcome. I better get going. See ya around, Eliza." She placed the tinfoil-wrapped plate in my arms and walked away.

"She seems like a nice girl," Mom commented after she had closed the door.

"Okay, sure," I replied. "But right now can you show me the way back up to my room? I want to get a bit more time to snooze. I'm exhausted."

Chapter Two

The next day I decided I would go and explore. Explore everything: the house, the yard, and the neighborhood.

The house was really pretty, two stories high, not including the basement and the creepy attic. There were cherry stairs, cabinets, paneling and floors. The kitchen was open, bright and sunny. In the kitchen there was a smooth blue granite countertop, a fridge, stove, microwave, oven, sink, dishwasher, and some more cabinets. The dining room was attached to the kitchen and was simple and sweet. A table with some chairs sat in the middle of the room, and some small paintings of flowers were scattered here and there on the wall. There was a screen door to let in air. The den here on the East Coast is called a family room. The "family room" was big and spacey, and, of course, soon filled up with Poppy and Sydney's toys. There were a lot of big windows. The furniture was soft and elegant. There was a computer, two small coffee tables, a television, and even some more cabinets! The study was strictly off-limits for the twins because my parents worked in there.

I ran down the steps of the front porch. There was a porch swing. Nice.

The neighborhood was old-fashioned and quaint. It was like something out of one of my plays, just like my parents said. I wondered where that Ollie Barnes's house was, but I wasn't going to look for it right now.

The grass in the yard was a healthy shade of green, with some small pine trees. I quickly realized I had been right to wear my sneakers out. The grass was still dewy and wet, even if it wasn't the morning anymore. There was a white picket fence surrounding the lawn. There was also a seesaw, much to Poppy and Sydney's delight, so the previous owners must have had kids.

I wandered around, poking and prodding, looking for somewhere where I could write my latest play. Should I lean against the corner of the fence? Eh. Might not be so comfortable. Sit behind that bush over there? I tried it. *I don't think so!* I attempted to come out, but a twig caught at my long wavy hair. I grimaced and gently untangled my hair from the branch.

Light bulb!

(Okay, I know I'm a dork, but I liked that movie *Despicable Me*, all right? It was funny when the main character would say "*Liiight bulllb,*" in that silly accent. But for the record, Poppy and

Sydney dragged me to see it. I didn't see it of my own accord!)

There were a few trees in the yard…great for climbing! I surveyed them all. Too high. Too many branches. Not sturdy enough. And then finally I found the right tree. It was a tree with about seven thick branches, with leaves on it, but not so many that I couldn't get any sunlight. Just enough to give me some shade. I saw that a couple of branches were bent a little, kind of forming little seats. I also noted there was one branch right in the middle, so I could hold on to that when I was sitting. This was a perfect tree!

I ran inside to get some of my special lined paper and an erasable pen. I have to use these materials when I am writing a script or else I can't focus. Of course, I also use colored yarn, but only when I am done. I tied the holes of the papers together, making what looked like script booklets.

To answer your question, yes, I *am* a playwright. I don't care if somebody thinks it's cool and somebody thinks it's incredibly stupid. I am what I am. Fun fact: William Shakespeare, one of the world's most well-known people, was a playwright. Okay, sorry, everybody knows that. But anyway, I wrote plays depending on my mood: If I were happy, I wrote a play where the theme was very light and comic. If I were sad, I wrote an awful tragedy. If I were feeling bold, I wrote a play where the characters go on a grand adventure. Today, I was feeling like an adventure.

I hoisted myself up onto the tree and sat down on one of the arced branches. It was absolutely perfect! I started to write.

Scene One
(Azalea and Dawn enter the stage. Two mysterious figures appear out of shadow and chain Azalea and Dawn's hands together.)
Azalea   &   Dawn: AHHHHHH!!!!!!!!! (They shout for help.)
Azalea: You stop that!
Dawn: Unchain my hands right now!
Azalea: You better stop NOW! (Starts flailing wildly; kicking and lashing out.)
(The girls try to shout more for help, but the mysterious men take bandanas and wrap them around A & D's noses and mouths. Before they wrap

them around their faces, Azalea screams-)

Azalea: If I smother in this it'll be your fault!

Dawn: (hysterically) What the heck?! Don't you dare!

(Mysterious men drag the girls up to top of very tall tower. They thrust the girls in a small, circular room with nothing in it. They unwrap bandanas and take off chains.)

Azalea & Dawn: WHAT ARE YOU DOING AND WHO ARE YOU?

Men: (chuckling darkly) Oh, you'll see.

(Men click the lock of the door behind them.)

Scene Two

I settled my papers together. That would be enough for one day. Like a monkey, I swung down from the tree.

I was already pretty sure of who would play my characters. Poppy and Sydney would be hilarious as the mysterious men, and I'd planned all along to play Azalea myself. But who would be Dawn? And the evil queen?

A sudden burst of Poppy-and-Sydney giggles from the house startled me. Then more laughter, then shrieking.

"E-WIZA! E-WIZA!"

I dropped the manuscript and scrambled indoors.

"Did you leave the screen door open?" demanded Mom.

"Uh…no?"

I looked down at the floor. There was Sydney, cupping something in her hands, tears streaming down her face. There was Poppy, trying to block my father from getting to her twin sister. She was puffing and her face was red.

"What's going on?"

"Don't go off topic. Young lady, tell me the truth. Did you leave the screen door open?"

"Um, maybe?" I tried.

Mom glared at me.

"Possibly? Okay, fine, it's entirely possible."

Wait. Why would she care? Normally it didn't matter so much.

I dropped to my knees to inspect the situation. Sydney seemed to be holding something brown and white.

Something moving. I gasped.

"E-wiza!" Poppy screamed. "Help me!"

"E-wiza, they are gonna take Cow away! Stop them, E-wiza!" Sydney hugged the thing to her chest.

"Eliza Brooke Hawthorne! You will do no such thing!" Mom said.

"Mom, Dad, I think I know how to calm them down." I took a deep breath. "Maybe you guys could just leave the room while I talk to them?"

My parents understood, even if Mom was sullen about it. Dad gave me a grateful glance. I don't think Poppy is the most reluctant when it comes to wrestling, um, if you know what I mean.

"Okay," I said. "So, who's going to give me the scoop?"

"Cow came in here when you left the door open," Poppy said matter-of-factly.

"Who's Cow?"

Sydney opened her arms a little. I could not believe my eyes. Clutched in Sydney's sticky arms was a rabbit.

Oh. My. Gosh. What had they done?

"Mommy and Daddy got all mean and said we have to give Cow back to the n-nature! But Cow is me and Poppy's bunny!" Sydney looked extremely worried. "So we had to protect her."

They were smart for their age. Poppy was definitely the fiercer twin, so she'd guard the rabbit.

Sydney was the gentler twin, so she'd hold "Cow." It was a good strategy. I bit my tongue to keep from laughing, even though this wasn't that funny.

"Why is her name Cow?" I asked.

"She looks like a cow," Poppy and Sydney both said together. She kind of did, with her brown fur and white splotches. "She looks like the cow at the zoo in Ca-wifornia," Poppy added.

I shook my head and rolled my eyes when the twins weren't looking. Poppy whispered something to her sister. Sydney nodded.

"Wanna hold Cow?" Poppy said, putting on her most angelic face.

Eek. Sure, Cow was cute, but she was a wild animal. She might even have rabies. *But*, I figured, looking at the drowsy bunny, *probably not.*

I held out my arms. Sydney carefully plopped the animal in them.

Cow was warm, and her stomach went in and out as she breathed. She shifted her position in my arms and then fell asleep. You had to admit she was adorable, but I highly doubted my parents would take in a rabbit.

"Well…" I looked over at my sisters. Big mistake. They were looking at me with such hopeful expressions I knew I just couldn't let them down. They thought I could do anything. "How about you guys go up to your room for a little while so I can talk to Mommy and Daddy about keeping her? She just needs to be with me while I do this, okay?"

Their faces lit up like the light displays on the buildings in San Francisco during the wintertime. Sydney gave me a wobbly grin. Poppy tugged impatiently on her hand and the two of them scurried upstairs.

Well, I thought, *here goes nothing.*

I walked into the family room. Cow woke up and wiggled her ears. Cute Cow. I stroked her with a finger and cooed, "Rise and shine, Cowie. This is going to be a big day!"

Chapter Three

Lucky Cow, I thought as I stared at all the brightly patterned carpets in the department store. *She doesn't have to decide what goes on the bottom of her cage. Just newspaper.*

"Eliza? Have you picked out a carpet yet?" Dad asked.

"The twins are getting impatient, honey," Mom reminded me. "They already picked theirs."

"We have names, you know," Poppy said. She made a face.

"You do?" I said crabbily. If there's one thing I hate, it's being rushed.

"Uh huh! My name's Sydney, and hers is Poppy!" Sydney looked concerned, as if she thought I actually forgot her name.

I moved over to a different display. This pile seemed better. I selected a small blue, red and purple rug.

"You don't want a wall-to-wall carpet?" Dad said.

"I like the wood floor."

We paid for the rug and walked out of the carpet section of the store. Time for beds.

First we looked at the little kid beds. Poppy and Sydney instantly chose a pink bunk bed with a slide for when you come down. CHILD-PROOF, a sticker on the bed said. Duh. There was also a little set of stairs for getting up. They picked out two bedspreads with different colored hearts and butterflies.

My bed took a little longer. I found a cute bedspread with stripes in practically every color of the rainbow - especially purple, my favorite color. There were some deep purple stripes, violet ones, lilac ones, and some lavender ones. There were also blue sheets that I liked.

I finally found a good bed. It was made of a dark, dramatic wood - *oak,* I thought. I was content, even though I felt a little grumpy.

Next up, extra stuff.

I picked a lamp with a purple shade and little blue beads at the end. It was pretty, I had to admit. I also picked a desk with lots of drawers and a swivel chair. My dresser, purple fuzzy beanbag chair, and shelf from San Francisco would remain, to my relief. In the hardware store I chose a light, light sky blue paint.

It was all nice, I decided, walking out of the store with my family. But it was never going to be as pretty as my room back in California.

I had second thoughts once we redecorated my

new room.

● ●

I was working on my Azalea-Dawn play. It was really suspenseful -- at least I thought so. These two girls were trapped in a tower together, and they had to figure a way out. There was a mean queen who plotted an evil scheme to keep them locked in. I was about to erase a stupid line I wrote, but somebody shouted my name first.

"E-wiza!"

I hopped down from my tree and ran inside. I desperately hoped Poppy and Sydney hadn't found another wild animal. Cow was enough work as it was.

"Yeah?" I asked Sydney. Poppy was holding the phone. She put her hand on the receiver, something she had seen Mom do.

"Aw-wee Barnes wants to talk with you," Sydney said in a hushed whisper.

I let out a small groan. "Okay, Pop, hand me the phone."

"Hello?" a girl's voice asked. "Is this Eliza?"

"Yeah. Hi," I said.

"Hi, Eliza! This is Ollie Barnes. You know, I live a few houses down from you? I dropped off those pancakes the other day? So, I'm just wondering if you'd want to come to my house today."

"Uh, okay, sure." My heart sank. I wanted to say no, but I couldn't. How can you when someone is being so friendly?

"Great! Can you come in ten minutes?"

"Sure," I said. *Wow,* I thought, *great vocabulary, Eliza.*

"See you then!" And with that, Ollie hung up.

Eleven minutes and thirty-seven seconds later, I was trudging down the block, wearing my tan corduroy jacket that I think makes me look like a girl detective. I was also carrying Cow's cage.

"Hi!" Ollie answered the door almost immediately.

I faked a smile. "Thanks for inviting me."

Ollie shrugged. "No problem. Come on in."

Ollie's house was structured the same way as mine, only her bedroom was in their attic.

I loved Ollie Barnes's bedroom. The wood floor, walls, and ceiling were really shiny and smooth. Her bed was a bunk bed, only there was one bed on it. Where the lowest bed should have been there was a desk, cluttered with arts-and-crafts supplies. There was a funky, swirly metal mobile. If you spun the mobile gently, it looked like the big light purple glass ball was sliding down, though it really wasn't. There was a colorful painting hanging

27

on the wall. It looked as if a rainbow was shining into her room, even though it was super small.

"What are you holding?" Ollie said, motioning to Cow's cage.

"Oh, this is my sisters' and my rabbit, Cow." I said, plucking the legendary bunny out of her cage. Cow opened one eye sleepily. I kissed her long ear.

"She's really cute!" Ollie exclaimed. "Where'd you get her?"

I told Ollie the hilarious story of Cow's breaking-and-entering into our house. She thought it was really funny, and soon we were both cracking up. She got a bit more serious when I told her how hard it was to convince my parents that Cow wouldn't be able to live in the wild; she'd fall asleep and a predator would eat her up in a snap. Cow needed a good home.

Suddenly, like lightning, I had a quick thought. *I liked Ollie.* She was clever and fun to be with. She wasn't boring, and she had a great imagination. Even though I didn't really know her all that well yet, anyone could tell we'd become good friends.

I think that was when I started to like my new home.

"Come on, Eliza, come meet my family." Ollie stood up. "You can leave Cow here."

I put Cow back in her cage and then followed Ollie down the two flights of stairs.

"Hungry?" Ollie said. She opened the refrigerator and tossed a circle of foil to me. She took another one for herself.

"What is this?" I unwrapped the circle and a delicious smell filled the kitchen.

"Wemmonkukeez," Ollie replied. Her mouth was already crammed with something.

"Huh?" I was completely bewildered.

Ollie gulped. "Lemon cookies!" she said, laughing. "My mom has her own line of treats. It's called -- "

"Hi, Eliza!" A woman with dirty-blond curls entered the room. "I'm Tara Barnes. I'm Ollie's mother. You know, Ollie's been looking forward to you moving to the block."

Ollie blushed. I giggled.

Tara Barnes turned to her daughter. "What were you saying to Eliza, Ollie?"

"I was telling her about the Sweet Apron. That's the name of my mom's pastry shop," Ollie explained. "We were eating some leftover lemon cookies."

As if to make her point, she unwrapped the second lemon cookie in her hands and took a generous bite. I took a polite nibble of mine, just to see if I liked it. I normally don't think citrus and sugar go that well together, but this was simply scrumptious. "Mmmm..." I said. I smacked my tongue against my lips. "It's great, Mrs. Barnes!" I exclaimed.

"Glad you think so." And with a laugh, Mrs. Barnes left the kitchen.

"Your mom's a really good cook," I told Ollie.

She grinned. "I know. Actually, I'm a big help around the house. Since I have such a sweet tooth, I always get rid of leftovers quickly!"

We wandered into the study, where Ollie's father, a happy looking man with laugh crinkles around his glasses-framed eyes, was talking on the phone. Ollie put her finger to her lips in the *shush* sign. Mr. Barnes waved, and gave us a thumbs-up before motioning for us to get out.

We were walking in the hallway now. The floor was wood and shiny, and very slippery. There was a little boy on the stairs, engrossed in a sound machine toy. *Beep, beep, beep. Hey, you! Wheee-oooo-wheee-oooo! Ring-a-ling-a-ling!* There were noises on that thing from a car honking to a siren, from a gangster to a telephone. Ollie poked the boy.

"Max!" she said.

"What?" he mumbled. Max looked about four or five years younger than us. He glanced up at me, confusion on his face.

"Max, this is Eliza." Ollie said.

"Hi," was Max's distracted answer. *Gurgle, gurgle,* went the sound machine.

Ollie rolled her eyes. "Max turned six a few months ago. See, he gets the short name. Just three letters! And I get a whole, long, fancy name. Who's ever heard of an eleven-year-old girl named Olympia? It sounds like an old lady's name," she complained.

Max snickered. Ollie noogied him. "You little cutie," she said affectionately. Max glared at her, and pressed a button on the sound machine. *Ahhhhhh!* it screamed. He picked it up and ran away, his own yell mingling with his sound machine's. "Olympia's weird! Olympia's weird! She's an old lady!"

"Max!" Ollie said, sighing. "That kid drives me crazy."

"Have you met my twin sisters yet?" I said, smiling.

"Do you know how to sock-skate?" Ollie asked. She had blue and green polka-dotted white socks, I noticed.

I smiled, and looked down at my own red striped socks. "Duh. I used to live in an apartment where there was practically no carpeting, you know," I told her.

"Where'd you move from?" Ollie asked.

I frowned. For a minute there I had forgotten I had only known Ollie for approximately two hours.

"I...I lived in San Francisco," I said softly,

looking at the floor. But Ollie could still hear the sorrow in my voice. My eyes stung.

"Do you miss it?" Ollie looked me in the eye. Her sympathetic blue eyes comforted me only a little. She touched my arm. I flinched slightly.

"Yes," I whispered.

I expected Ollie to say "I'm sorry," but she didn't. I was grateful for that, because people had said that to me before. I'd wanted to shout at them, "Don't say that! It isn't your fault! Stay out of it!" Ollie didn't try to change the subject. I think she knew that if I wanted to talk about it, she should let me. *That was nice of her,* I thought briefly.

"Well?" I wiggled my socked foot. "Do you want to sock-skate or what?"

We glided across the hall. In case you don't know what sock-skating is, it is when you wear socks and pretend you're skating. You need a wooden floor, or at least a smooth, non-carpeted floor.

We sock-skated for a long time. So long that my feet started to hurt. So long that Ollie bumped into the wall. Laughing, I crashed into Ollie and fell on the floor, and I finally knew it was time to go home.

Chapter Four

No, no, sound more, um, mysterious, more evil!" I groaned.

Ollie Barnes, Poppy, Sydney, and I were practicing my play. I was Azalea, Ollie was Dawn, and Poppy and Sydney were the mysterious men. The twins were very emotional actors - but more in an I'm-so-innocent way, not an I'm-so-evil way.

"All right, guys, from the top," I ordered. Ollie and I screamed.

"You stop that!" I yelled.

"Unchain my hands right now!" Ollie said.

"You better stop now!"

We screamed some more.

"If I smother in this it'll be your fault!"

"What the heck? Don't you dare!"

We went on until the twins' first line. The twins tried to chuckle darkly, but it was really more of a giggle.

"Ho, huh, ha, ho," I pronounced. "Kind of like that."

"Ho, huh, ha, ho! You'll see."

We ran through the entire scene.

"Okay, Poppy, Sydney, thanks. You can go

back to what you were doing now," I said.

Ollie and I went inside to get our bathing suits. We were going to go swim in the Lake, a.k.a. Minnow Pond.

"What is school like?" I asked. "I mean, going to Sparrow Middle?"

"Well, I'm only entering Sparrow Middle in the fall. I just finished fifth grade, you know."

"Yeah, I know, I did too. But the buildings are kind of connected, right?"

"Uh huh. Sparrow Elementary is okay. I'm not sure how much I'm going to like middle school. I heard you get a lot of homework. I even have homework to work on during the summer, and I only just finished fifth grade," Ollie replied.

I beamed. I didn't have any summer work. They don't give you any when you're moving across the country.

"Who are your friends?" We ran into my bedroom.

On the walk there, Ollie said thoughtfully, "Well, I like Laura Hayes, and Janie Kippers-"

"Wha - ?" A girl riding her bike almost crashed into us. "Oops, sorry, hi, Ollie!"

"Hey, Jeanna," Ollie said, smiling. "This is Eliza. She's new in my neighborhood, and she'll be at Sparrow Middle with us."

Jeanna flashed me a winning smile. She had

34

perfect, white teeth.

"Hi. My name is Jeanna. That's J-E-A-N-N-A. It's pronounced *Gina*. When I'm older I'm going to change the spelling to G-I-N-A. I think it sounds a bit more professional, don't you?"

Ollie's smile looked a little strained now. Jeanna looked me up and down. "Have you ever seen the movies *The Ruby Ring* or *My Only Sunshine*?"

"No," I said, puzzled. "Why?"

"My mother's the star in both. You know, Juliette Lemmonhart," she urged. I think she expected me to say "Ah, yes, I know," or nod with recognition.

"Who?" I said bluntly.

"Well, she's a famous actress. I would really watch those movies if I were you. They're fabulous."

"Okay, sure," I said.

"Nice meeting you, Chuck. See you around, Ollie!" And with that, Jeanna Lemmonhart rode her pink bike away.

"Chuck?" I said, looking around. "Who's Chuck?"

"You, silly," Ollie said. "She likes Peanuts a lot. Small world, huh?"

Ollie paused.

"She's really nice once you get to know her,"

she said slowly, making sure I understood.

"Yeah," I nodded. "There was a girl at my old school like that. Her dad was a really well-known comedian or something." I pictured Jordi Halter's smooth reddish-brown hair and hawk-like cinnamon eyes, kind before Jordi only seemed angry when she looked at me. "She was really nice to me. Before, um, I moved, I mean."

Ollie nodded. Then she exclaimed, "Hey, look, we're here!"

It was my first time at the Lake (Minnow Pond). It was actually my first time swimming in a lake since I was, like, five. There are no lakes in San Francisco. Sure, there's the Pacific Ocean, but really we only went to the beach if it was extremely hot out, which was very rare. The Pacific is nearly always below sixty degrees – brrr! Cold!

The Lake was wonderful. There was yellowish-white sand up until the water started, where you put your beach chairs and towels and stuff. There was a tilted ramp to get to the water. There was a floating dock in the deepest part of Minnow Pond that people were allowed to swim in. The rest of the Lake was roped off for boats and jet-skis. The Lake's surface was a shimmering dark green color that made everything seem peaceful and undisturbed. *But,* I thought a second later, *maybe that's because no one's here except us today.*

Everything looked like it belonged on a postcard.

"Most people think it's cold," Ollie warned me. We walked across the sand to get to the water. We stepped in, our ankles submerged in greenish freshwater. They looked cut by the water's surface.

Ollie sighed contentedly. "*I* just think it's refreshing!"

I giggled. "Me too!" I waded in farther. Now the water was up to my knees. I swam deeper and deeper until my whole body was underwater, except my head.

"Last one to the dock is a rotten egg!" Ollie yelled.

We swam as fast as our legs would allow us. While I was swimming, I swallowed a huge mouthful of lake water, causing me to sputter and cough. While Ollie was swimming, something long and slimy brushed past her legs, and she screamed. We quickly stopped to find out it was just a huge leaf. I eventually beat Ollie to the dock, but only by a few seconds.

We climbed on top of the dock. I stretched out and laid down in the sunlight, cold from swimming in the Lake. Ollie just sat on the edge, dangling her feet in the water. She was unusually quiet, and I noticed a sly look overcoming her face.

"What are you up to?" I asked her suspiciously.

Ollie didn't answer. Instead, she tipped the

dock over! I found myself treading water in the deepest, blackest, murkiest part of the Lake.

"Not fair!" I growled, giggling. I started to chase her.

"Oh, Eliza!" Ollie pointed to some huge rocks sitting in very shallow water. "Let's go over there."

I scowled but followed her lead. Ollie sat on one of those massive rocks. I did too. The surface of the smooth, small boulder was hot and felt very soothing. I yawned.

"Eliza?"

I blinked. "Mmmm?"

"Do you want to make mud pies? That's why we're over here."

"Huh? Um, sure," I said, yawning again.

Ollie snapped her fingers in front of my eyes. "Wake up, sleepyhead!"

She bent down and scooped up some of the muddy sand at the bottom of the water. I copied her.

"Take out rocks or anything you find in the sand," she instructed. "They'll make good toppings later."

The wetness of the mud felt squishy in my fingers. It was also a weird color, a mix between beige and gray. I played with it, flicking it everywhere.

"Stop!" Ollie said, laughing. She wiped some mud off her pink, black, and white Speedo one-piece.

I took another handful of sand. "What do I do now?"

"Mold it," Ollie said. She took some more sand and shaped it into a half-circle and put it on the rock we had been sitting on. I did the same.

"Pinch the edges, like this. Then find things, toppings, I mean, to put on your pie. It can be anything, really."

We searched all over the Lake, on the (dry) sand, and in the rough grasses that were near the water. I scrounged up a few red pebbles, two white pebbles, one green rock, and a black feather with some white stripes at the top. Ollie revealed a scraggly-looking weed, a couple of pine needles, and some more pebbles. We decorated our mud pies and admired them from a distance.

Ollie smiled. "Aren't they a gross color? My mom says that mud should be a different color, because she thinks no pie should look like that."

"We could color them with food coloring," I joked.

Ollie's face lit up. "Yeah!" she said. "Maybe tomorrow! My mom has lots of colors!"

I mentally slapped myself. "Ollie, don't you think your mom will want to keep it for her recipes? Is it allowed?"

"Don't worry." Ollie shrugged. "It's just food

coloring. I'll ask my mom if I can take it."

I moaned.

● ●

The next day, I found myself at the Barnes's front step, ringing the doorbell.

"One minute, Eliza, honey!" came Mrs. Barnes's voice.

Mrs. Barnes opened the door. She was holding a glass plate in her hands. "Hi, Eliza! How are you? Ollie will be down in a minute. Try this, would you?"

She gave me a golden cookie. I popped it in my mouth. "Delicious!" I told her. "What is it?"

"Apple-cinnamon. Like it? It's a new recipe."

"Yeah, it's great!" *Mmmm.* The taste of the cinnamon lingered in my mouth.

"Thank you, dear. Here, bring these to your family, too." She placed the plate in my hands.

Ollie came running down the stairs. She held a striped bag. "Hey, Eliza! I've got the food coloring. Mom, I'll be back around eleven o'clock. Bye, see you later!"

"Thanks for the cookies," I added politely.

We quickly dashed to my house to give my parents and sisters the cookies. The twins answered the door, wearing dinosaur costumes and my mother's high heels. They instantly attacked the cookies.

We didn't run into Jeanna Lemmonhart again, much to my relief. Ollie and I chattered on and on about everything. From the way we talked, any passerby would think we had known each for a really long time or we were twins, but twins that weren't identical. I have freckles and I'm tall and dark-haired, and Ollie's smaller and has shorter blond hair. But we both have the same blue eyes.

We arrived at the Lake, Ollie still swinging the striped bag that I suspected held the coloring. She dumped the contents on the sandy, beach-like part of the Lake property. My suspicions were confirmed. Out tumbled five tiny plastic bottles, each containing jewel-bright liquid.

"We have red, blue, green, purple, and orange," Ollie said.

"Come on," I said to Ollie. She scooped up the bottles and together we waded through the shallow water to the big boulder where our mud pies still sat patiently. They looked a little more squashed than they had the day before.

We opened the bottles and I was surprised at how messy the dye could become. I even got green food coloring on my purple and white bathing suit. We were very careful not to get food coloring in the Lake's water, because we weren't one hundred percent sure that food coloring was terrific for the fish and gulls to eat.

We dyed each pie a different color. Some were tie-dye. It looked so weird and beautiful at the same time. Rainbow muck. I smiled.

"Isn't it cool how any ordinary thing can be beautiful?" I asked Ollie, not even sure what I was saying, glancing up at the glaring late morning sun. "Like, gross mud can be turned a bright color?"

Ollie changed her sitting position on the rock. She seemed to be pondering my question.

"And how this red food coloring isn't just red, it's...scarlet! And the purple is violet, and the orange is kind of the color of the outside of a blood orange. Green is pine, and the blue is really more of a turquoise."

Ollie laughed. "Turquoise mud pies!"

I smiled and looked up at the sun again.

Chapter Five

I pressed my face against the window, searching for my friend Ollie. I took the phone and dialed her cell phone number.

"Hello?" Ollie's voice sounded high and squeaky over the phone.

"Ollie, it's me. You sound like a chipmunk! Where are you? I've been looking for you all day!" As soon as the words left my mouth, I blushed crimson. I wish I had not mentioned the chipmunk thing. But Ollie just laughed cheerfully, and I felt relieved. Another great quality about Ollie was that she was always laughing and very hard to offend.

"Eliza! Um, I'm at one of my family friend's house, and I'm gonna be there the rest of the day. We're having dinner with them."

"Oh."

"I know. It stinks, right?" she said teasingly.

"Yeah, it really does," I replied, disappointment in my voice.

"But wasn't there something you wanted to do that you told me a couple days ago? Plant your garden or something?"

"Oh yeah! Thanks, Barol." Barol was my code

name for Ollie. My code name was Hawel. I won't tell you the trick. Figure it out yourself by looking at our first and last names.

I could tell Ollie was grinning over the phone. "'Welcome, Hawel. Gotta run, my mom's wondering where I went."

I hung up the phone and rushed upstairs to get some necessities for gardening: a black sweatshirt, sneakers, a gardening spade, gardening gloves, and seed packets.

As I rushed outside, I gazed at my plant tools with affection. I hadn't taken these out in such a long time, not since I was little, when I grew to love gardening like my dad. At first, up until I was - I think - three, I stuck to the basics. I put the soil and seeds in the flower pots inside the house. When I was four, Dad taught me how to take care of my plants while gardening outside. I was awed by the tiny seeds. I was no older than Poppy and Sydney then.

Last year, I took a free botany class at the library, and I did my fifth grade science fair project on a plant's growth. It turned out nicely, thank you very much, with the little sprouts displayed next to my poster board. Karynn had said it was pretty cool, and Jordi had gushed on and on about how I had a way with plants. Angela, the quietest of our group, had complimented me and said that my project was really official looking.

I remembered this with some confusion. At first I was smiling, and then I frowned. Jordi and Karynn weren't that nice to me anymore. Just because I had to move! I scoffed at their ridiculousness. Last week I had received a short but sweet postcard from Angela. It had all the boring, typical stuff in it.

I frowned again. Jordi, Karynn, and Angela were no longer my best friends. Who was, then? I didn't really know anybody in Sparrow except…

Ollie. Ollie? Ollie Barnes? Could she be my best friend? I wasn't sure, but she was a close friend of mine. For the rest of the summer I thought hard about this question.

Eliza, get a grip. You're trying to find a nice patch of soil for your seeds, remember? I thought. I finally found a wide rectangular area. Oh, I was so happy to be gardening again, though I didn't realize I was thinking that. In California there was just no space. The only exception was the science fair, but that was indoors.

I scooped up some soil in my cupped, gloved hands. I sighed with delight. I loved the feeling of the rich, dark earth slipping through my fingertips. I took the seed packets and examined the print carefully. **Tulips,** one read. There was a picture of iridescent flowers above. **Carnations**, read

45

another, with a picture of those frilly, familiar flowers. I had lots more flower seeds, but only one type of vegetable and herb seeds. I had snap pea seeds, because snap peas were my favorite green food, and this herb that I'd nicknamed the lemon plant before I'd learned how to spell my own name. It had a real scientific name, only I forgot it. It was a clover-like plant, and you plucked off the leaves and chewed on them until they were gross and soggy. They tasted lemony for the first few minutes.

I took some tulip seeds and buried them in the dirt just the way my father taught me. The flowers had their own part of the soil patch, separate from the lemon plant and the snap peas.

Poppy and Sydney came running out of the house, holding Cow, who had been stuffed into one of Poppy's old ballerina tutus. She looked adorable and...sleepy, like she always did. Oh, good ol' Cow.

"Hi, E-wiza!" the twins said. They hadn't been able to pronounce some of their tricky *l*'s for a long time, in case you're wondering. "Whatcha doing?" Poppy asked, leaning closer to my soil patch.

"I'm gardening, Pop," I said, not even looking up.

"What are you planting?" said Sydney shyly.

"Okay, here are tulips, there are carnations right here, and daisies over here. I have to plant the rest of the flowers, but over there are snap peas and this thing called a lemon plant."

"What's a wemon plant?" Poppy said, her tongue stumbling over all the *l*'s.

Okay, the twins were being kind of irritating now.

"You'll see, Poppy," I said, trying to sound cheerful and completely un-annoyed. Poppy and Sydney would be upset if they saw I was annoyed with them. Whenever they get on my nerves, they go into hysterics trying to be nice and perfect little sisters. Please don't ask me why, because I have no clue.

"Okay!" both twins said at the same time. Honestly, I bet if I slapped Poppy in the face, Sydney could feel it, and if I slapped Sydney, Poppy would feel it. It's like they have this twin bond or something. They're best friends and probably will always be.

They put Cow in her cage beside me on the grass, and scurried off to the seesaw.

I planted the rest of the flowers and stood up, brushing dirt off my jeans. "Most of the plants should start growing next week!" I called to Poppy and Sydney.

Cow looked up at me mournfully. I picked up her cage and went inside.

"Well, what do we do now, Cow?" I sighed.

Cow moved her plump little paw, as if she was beckoning me to come and stroke her. Cow had been scrawny and thin when the twins first discovered her, but we'd made sure she ate a lot after taking her to the vet and getting her shots.

Outside, the sky was quickly turning stormy gray. Soon, it started to drizzle, and then a downpour. *Good*, I thought, *water for my flowers and plants*. Poppy and Sydney were inside as soon as the first flash of lightning struck the ground, wet to the bone and shivering. I immediately went upstairs to get soft towels for them.

I picked out Poppy and Sydney's favorite towels, the pink and purple striped ones. I ran downstairs, the towels flying out like a cape behind me. I handed them over and plopped down on the dark, cozy couch. Poppy and Sydney had a watercolor set in front of them.

"Hi, E-wiza," Poppy said pleasantly. "We are painting horses with corns."

Horses with corns? "You mean unicorns?" I asked.

Sydney smiled sweetly, her dimples appearing in her cheeks. "Sure."

I cleared my throat, trying not to laugh. The splotches on their papers were supposed to be unicorns?

I grinned wickedly. "Oh yeah? Well, let me

show you how the expert unicorn-painter paints unicorns."

I took the paper and watercolors from them and drew a wobbly, watery pink outline of a horse with a horn on the top of its head.

I wasn't very good at making people or animals with watercolors, though I was handy with the paintbrush because I could paint funky shapes and bright colors to look like a really cool painting. But Ollie loved art more than me. Ollie's and my parents together were looking into a fine arts sleep away camp for Ollie and me to go to next summer. This summer I couldn't go because things were crazy because of the move, and Ollie wasn't allowed until next year.

Until then, I would have to make do with adventures with Ollie, laughs with my sisters, short letters from Angela, conversations with my parents, my wonderful writing tree, my new garden, and what was in store.

● ●

I drummed my fingers across the granite countertop. I was so bored! The twins had lost interest in painting mythical horses, Ollie still wasn't back, I couldn't find the manuscript for my play to read over, and it was raining outside. The thunderstorm had calmed, and now it was only a slight drizzle. But it was the type of drizzle that drives you insane and stir-crazy, not the soothing pounding rain that makes you want to cuddle up in a fuzzy blanket.

I wondered what I should do to keep myself entertained. I decided to check up on sweet Cow. I sock-slid across the hall (with my new soft red-white-and-blue socks) to the twins' bedroom.

"Hey, Cow," I said, flopping down beside the cage in the marshmallow-pink-painted corner.

Cow was asleep.

ASLEEP!

I groaned. I felt dangerously tempted to wake her up, but I resisted. Instead, I braided some of my dark hair. After that, I got to my feet and trudged to *my* bedroom, where I flopped down in my purple beanbag chair. I started making a little friendship bracelet to weave into the wires of Cow's cage, for decoration.

I knew I should probably use pastel shades for a rabbit, even though rabbits don't wear friendship bracelets, but I was so stir-crazy I needed something bold and outgoing. I picked a shiny strand of gold which wasn't even string but would work anyway. And with that I picked hot tangerine, electric blue, lime green, highlighter yellow, and a warlike shade of violet.

After I finished, I went into the kitchen to find a bulky manila envelope with my name and address on it! I scanned the envelope to find the return address.

Angela!

Chapter Six

Angela's letter was one of the longest she had ever written to me, but it brought bad, bad, bad news.

Here it was:

Dear Eliza,

How are you? I'm okay, I guess. Jordi and Karynn are fine, just so you know.

Tell me more about Olympia. She sounds nice. I wish I could meet her! Does she have any pets? Are Poppy and Sydney friends with Max?

When does school start for you? For us, it starts August twenty-ninth. What's your school called?

So anyway, my mom was reading the paper the other day, and she found something upsetting. I read the article too. I thought that since you love Californian nature, you might want to read this.

I clipped it to the back of this letter.

XO,

Angela

I flipped over the page to find a clipping from the San Francisco Examiner. My eyes grew huge as I read the article.

The Governor of California insists upon cutting down record-setting Californian redwood trees in a park just outside the city of San Francisco and destroying natural habitat to construct more apartment buildings. Governor Corey says, "The San Francisco area must be successful in collecting property taxes from apartment complexes, office buildings and more. Cutting down just a little piece of the wilderness won't hurt."

My mouth dropped open.

Many San Franciscan residents have gathered on the sidewalks to protest, but our governor will not relent. "The elimination of the trees will take place from August 28th through October 1st," he says.

By Cecilia Herringbone

I let out a gasp. How could the governor be so cruel? I felt like I couldn't stand, so I collapsed onto a chair.

What was there to do?

I needed a plan.

Chapter Seven

And Ollie helped me think of one.

You see, she rushed over to my house the next day when I called, my voice urgent, about the redwood trees. I think she really understood how much it disturbed me, because I was half-crying on the phone. Anyway, when Ollie arrived, she was armed with a tissue box, old newspapers, glitter glue, squeaky Magic Markers, plain paper, Elmer's Glue, and brightly-colored poster boards. She was bending, clutching the materials so hard her knuckles were white.

"Hi," she said breathlessly. "I have some stuff."

"That's obvious! What did you bring with you? Attack of the art supplies…" My joke faded into nothing. I couldn't smile or laugh. Instead, I bent over, too, so I could help my friend carry everything.

Ollie stumbled a little. "Come on in," I said.

We walked upstairs. Ollie patted my back and said that we'd come up with the best idea (to save Californian wilderness) since canned tuna fish. I gave her a weird look at that one, and actually laughed.

Once we got to my bedroom - which had turned out looking awesome, mind you - she said, "Okay, Eliza. Get ready to think. We'll save those trees, and you know it! Now let's get to work!"

"Umm, I still don't understand why you brought a platoon of art supplies to my house," I replied, accidentally squeezing some silver glitter glue on my fingers.

"It's *not* a platoon - believe me, I have lots more stuff at home. I brought it so that when we come up with a plan soon, we can make whatever we need for it." She sighed with relief as she dropped everything on the small blue, red, and purple carpet in the middle of my room.

We sat for a couple minutes, the first ones in silence. Then I came up with an idea.

"How about we make friendship bracelets and sell them?" I asked. "I mean, both boys and girls wear friendship bracelets."

"I dunno, Eliza. The only friendship bracelet I've ever made was the one for you, when you taught me. And it came out really bad. I don't even know why you wear it."

I glanced fondly at the bright green, silver, and light purple woven bracelet on my wrist. "It isn't bad! And I wear it because you're my friend, plus I like it."

"Okay, okay, whatever you say," Ollie smiled. "But we aren't getting anywhere."

We sat thinking for a couple minutes more. Then the door creaked open. Poppy and Sydney's faces poked in. I winced. Couldn't my little sisters see this was a bad time?

"Mommy told us about the trees in Cawifornia," Poppy said, looking really upset.

"Uh-huh. Why are they doing it? E-wiza? Why?" Sydney said, staring up at me with huge blue eyes.

"It's okay, guys," said Ollie, who thought my sisters were soooooo cute.

"Aw-wee!" they shrieked at, apparently, Ollie. Poppy and Sydney ran over so they could sit on her lap and get comforted in this time of distress, but they tripped over some papers tied with yarn on my floor.

"Guys! Are you okay?" I said.

"Yes."

"Wait!" I ran over to the spot where they had fallen. "What did you trip over?" I crouched down, and picked up the manuscript of my play about Azalea and Dawn, which I had finished six days ago.

I groaned. The first page had a dirt smudge on it! I wasn't picky about germs, but I'd worked so hard.

Ollie had a reaction too, except hers was really different from mine. She gasped.

I craned my neck to see her expression. Her mouth was hanging open, and she looked like a lightning bolt had just struck her. I arched an eyebrow. What was up with Ollie?

Then it hit me too. I drew in my breath, sharply. "No!" I said. "No way!"

"Yes, Eliza! Why not? It's a perfect plan, you know it is."

"No, Ollie. I can't!"

Poppy and Sydney shared a look that clearly said, *What are they talking about? This is boring. No one's paying attention to us. Let's leave.* They tottered out into the hallway. Ollie and I didn't even notice.

"Eliza! Are you misreading my mind? Because what's going through my mind could work really well."

"No, I'm not misreading your mind. You want to perform my play to a bunch of strangers, and raise money so we can talk the governor out of ruining California. You know I'm shy about my play. I couldn't perform it in front of people!" Actually, this was an understatement. I was so self-conscious about Azalea and Dawn that only my sisters, my parents, Ollie, and Ollie's family knew about them and all the other characters in *Azalea*

57

and Dawn's Adventure.

"You're the bravest person I've met in my life. You're friendly even when you're uncomfortable, you're nice to your sisters even when they annoy you, and you're a loyal, fun, kind friend. You can do it!" Ollie said fervently.

I blinked.

"Oh no," I heard her say. "Oh, no, I'm being too pushy. You don't have to do it. It's fine. Just forget it, okay?"

"No," I said, my voice wavering. "No, it *is* a great idea." I swiped at my eyes, hard. "I'll do it, Ollie. What you just said wasn't pushy. It was really, really nice…" I paused, feeling really embarrassed. "And we'll definitely do this. I think we should start right away."

Ollie's eyes lit up. I could tell she was excited. So was I.

"I agree," she said, her curly blond hair bouncing on her shoulders, and she jumped up and down with excitement. "Let's begin."

● ●

We started by asking our parents. They thought it was a good start, but they didn't quite understand at first.

"Come on, Eliza, honey, don't you think it's a

bit impractical?" Mom asked gently. "I mean, we have to sell tickets, somehow find advertising…also, how would you get the money that you raise to the governor? You know how many aggravated people write to him in a day… you'd have to, what, basically set up a meeting with him to tell him what you did and everything… and Eliza, he lives in California!… not to mention where we would put on your little production?…"

"In our backyard!" I exclaimed, feeling a tiny bit stung from her calling my play a "little" thing. "And my 'little' production is actually *sixty* pages long."

My mom thought about performing it in my backyard for a while. She exchanged glances with my dad.

"I think it's okay, Laurie," Dad said slowly, glancing at me. "Think about all those walks through the redwoods we did back in California. I mean--" he paused, unsure what to say next.

My mom's face softened, no doubt remembering taking teensy babies (at the time) Poppy and Sydney and little first-grader Eliza to Muir Woods, Yosemite and Sequoia National Parks. *Redwood timber is in all of us, face it, Mom,* I pleaded in my head.

Still with that vague look on her face, Mom asked, "Well, what do Tara and Peter think about this?"

"I don't know. Ollie's talking to them about it right now. She promised she'd be back soon with results," I answered. *Whoops*. In the excitement, Ollie had left all the art supplies on my carpet. But that wasn't our worst problem right now.

Five minutes later, Ollie knocked on the door. I studied her face to see if her parents' input was negative or positive. But wait! Ollie had on a poker face. Argh! I wanted to kill her.

"Ollie...!" I yelled. "Tell me RIGHT now."

Ollie's petite face broke into a grin. Her blue eyes shone once more. I felt my body relax.

"Really? They said yeah?"

"Oh yes they did!" Ollie replied happily. Her cheeks flushed. "They only wanted to know if it was okay with your parents." She turned to my mom and dad. "Is it okay with you, Mr. and Mrs. Hawthorne?"

"Why not?" Dad said, while Mom said, "All right. If it's okay with your parents, Ollie, then...sure." But my mother still looked a little stressed out. Yikes. I suddenly realized that the twins' birthday was in, like, basically two weeks. And now we had dumped this on top of her.

"I promise you won't regret this, Mom!" I said happily. She gave me a smile in return.

I ran upstairs, pulling Ollie behind me.

Chapter Eight

I wrapped a piece of seaweed around a stick and stuck it in my blue mud pie. Ollie and I were relaxing at the shore of the Lake for a couple of hours. We just needed some time to think about our plan together. I wiped my hands on my bathing suit and headed up with Ollie to the sand to grab a snack.

As we munched on homemade marshmallow-y melting Rice Krispy Treats (courtesy of the Sweet Apron), we shared our thoughts aloud.

"We'll need costumes," I said pensively. "Do you know anyone who's really good at sewing?"

"Umm, not really. We'll have to figure that out. We also need some kids to play the other roles, like the mysterious men and the Evil Queen."

"Rats. I hadn't thought about the casting!"

We stared at each other. Then we sighed. I ran my finger up the pink stripe on my towel. Ollie said, "Eliza, I'm gonna go try and find the floaty tube I lost a couple days ago at the lost-and-found in the woods here. I'll be back soon."

As Ollie walked away, I waded back into the water. I swam up to the dock. I pulled myself up the ladder, huffing and puffing. I was about to sit down on the hard black surface when I realized I wasn't the only person there. Lying right next to me, working on a perfect tan, was a girl who looked around my age. She was wearing big sunglasses with sparkly silver frames.

"Hi!" I said, all friendly.

The girl sat up, took off her sunglasses, and looked me up and down. Huh. She looked kind of familiar. I wondered why?

The girl flipped her long honey brown fishtail braid to her back. She raised her eyebrows. "Do I know you?" Jeanna Lemmonhart asked in that funny accent.

"Yes!" I said. "Hi, Jeanna. I'm a friend of Ollie Barnes. I think we met once, briefly. Anyways, my name's Eliza."

"Oh!" Jeanna grinned. "I remember. Are you going to Sparrow Middle in September?"

"Uh-huh. I can't wait for sixth grade, can you?" I smiled at her. Sure, she was a teensy bit obnoxious, but I like making new friends, and really, I need all the new friends I can get in Sparrow for school this year.

"I know! I'm definitely going to try out for the plays they'll put on. I'm hoping they'll do *Wicked*. It's my all-time favorite."

I nodded, because I liked *Wicked* too. Jeanna

started singing "Popular," and I heard how pretty her voice was. And then I realized her mom was a superduperfamous movie star. And then I thought about how Jeanna had mentioned that she liked acting. And Ollie liked Jeanna, and I was warming up to her myself. And then I thought about my play.

Jeanna stopped singing and laid back down. "Do you have any pets?" she said. "I do. Her name is Raspberry. She's a French poodle, and she's so cute! A co-star in one of my mom's movies gave her to my mom a couple of years ago."

Even though Jeanna was a tiny bit self-absorbed, I liked her already. She reminded me of Jordi. Although if I moved (unlikely) I really hoped she wouldn't be unkind like my Californian ex-friend. And we needed somebody to play the Evil Queen. Desperately.

I saw Ollie walk over to our towels, gripping a huge water toy. She didn't see me, and she looked like she was going to start panicking any moment now if she couldn't find me.

I stood up on the raft, making it wobble. "OLLIE! OVER HERE!" I yelled to her.

Jeanna looked up from her monologue. "Oh, Ollie Barnes? I like her, we're friends at school. She's here?" Jeanna stood up too. "HI!"

Ollie swam over. "Oh my gosh, I was freaking out, Eliza! I was like, whoa, she disappeared!" She noticed Jeanna. "Hey, J.L.! How are you?"

"Hi, Ollie. I'm great, you? Awesome nails…" she replied, admiring Ollie's tie-dyed fingernails.

"Ollie, Jeanna likes acting," I said meaningfully. I eyed Ollie to see if she understood. She didn't.

"I know that." Ollie gave me a weird look. "Why'd you bring it up?"

"Umm…"

"Oooh!" Ollie understood now. She glanced at me. "Jeanna, can we ask you about something? Can we swim back up to shore?"

Jeanna was startled. "Okay, sure."

So we swam back to shore and Ollie and I confronted her about my play. We asked if she would like to play the Evil Queen.

"You think I'm mean enough to be her?" she said angrily, clearly offended. "Thanks a lot."

I was alarmed. Wow, this girl took stuff waaay too seriously.

"Ha ha, just kidding." She laughed, a cute tinkly sound. "Of course I'll do it. I would never turn down a good acting opportunity, plus I want to keep the redwoods in northern California too!"

Ollie hugged her. I, who thought it a little early in Jeanna's and my friendship for sudden hugging, slapped her a high-five.

"I'll make more copies of the script for you. As

soon as my parents finish editing it," I said to Jeanna.

We all slipped on our flip-flops and headed for the five-minute walk to my neighborhood. It gave me a chance to talk to Jeanna a little more, while Ollie, who seemed downright exhausted from swimming back and forth so many times, walked in quiet peacefulness.

"So," I said, "Where does your mom do her movies? I've never seen a movie studio around here."

"She lives in New York City. I live with my dad here. We Skype with her for half an hour every other night, and she comes and visits us a lot, like, every four weeks."

"If you don't mind answering my next question - "

"Not at all. Ask away. I'm used to questions."

"Well, are there any reasons why you don't live with your mom in NYC?" I blurted. *Ugh, that was SO rude of me!*

"How to start answering that question?" Jeanna wondered. "I mean, everybody knows that eleven years ago, famous Juliette Lemmonhart had a little baby girl in a hospital in London, right before she was about to shoot a movie taking place near Big Ben. It got so much publicity. Quite honestly, I can't remember, since I was a baby, but there are lots of clippings in my baby photo album from nice articles in the newspaper, with pictures of cute little baby me." She frowned. "Some articles weren't so kind. Apparently, the paparazzi were constantly taking awful pictures of me, and sometimes also my mom and dad. They would photograph me throwing a fit, or making a weird face, or burping, or…you get the idea. Daddy threw those pictures in the fireplace on one cold night in New York, because, you know, that was where Mom lived at the time, and she still does. And of course the movie producers called off the Big Ben movie as soon as she had me." She paused. "Are you getting all this?"

I winced a little. "Yeah, go on."

"So, to protect me from all the paparazzi, we moved to Sparrow, a small town nothing at all like New York. And Mom has made it clear that if the paparazzi try still to chase after me, they'll surely have to have a nice talk with the police. Because it's our private life, you know, and we can't have the press butting in at every minute."

"Wow," I remarked.

"I remember the first time you told me that!" Ollie said cheerfully, but tiredly. "It was on your first day of first grade."

I felt really grateful, then. I felt so grateful that I had a friend like Ollie who wouldn't get jealous if

I tried to make friends with another person, along with her. Jordi, Karynn and sometimes Angela would all not be that friendly to me for a whole twenty-four hours if I tried befriending a new kid at Golden Gate Bridge School, because they were jealous. Ollie was the nicest person somebody could ever know. Way nicer than my mean Californian friends.

We arrived at my street, and Ollie and I had to go back inside our houses - it was almost dinnertime - so Jeanna said goodbye and kept on walking to her house.

At dinner, I told my parents the good news.

"Great! You needed more kids to be in your show," Mom said.

"Maybe Jeanna will attract more ticket-buyers," Dad said, "since she's the daughter of a movie star."

"Uh huh," I said distractedly. My weariness had finally caught up with me, so I focused on getting slippery pesto pasta onto my fork.

● ●

The dot next to Ollie's screen name was green, so I clicked it.

redwoodgirl23: hey

ollietreat27: sup? :-)

redwoodgirl123: nuthin much, u?

ollietreat27: same here. im so bored

redwoodgirl123: kno the feeling

ollietreat27: my parents said yes to jeanna being in the play. yay!!

redwoodgirl123: mine 2 :-D

ollietreat27: jeanna is online rite now. want me 2 invite her 2 our chatroom??

redwoodgirl123: sure. i like her

jeannastar62 has joined

jeannastar62: hey ollie, eliza. wassup

ollietreat27: hi j.l.!

redwoodgirl23: hey jeanna.

redwoodgirl23: like your lines so far?

jeannastar62: yeah, they're fab! i got2go,guys. talk 2 u l8r.

ollietreat27: me 2. ttyl eliza

redwoodgirl23: k. bye

I snapped my laptop shut. I threw on my pajamas and yelled downstairs, "'Night, Mom, Dad, Poppy, and Sydney!"

"Good night, love you!" they all chorused back. And yes, I was so tired that I was going to bed before my little sisters.

I pulled my thick comforter (nights in the Berkshires really *were* chilly) over my head and snuggled in. I was truly exhausted, just like Ollie, and I had no trouble at all falling asleep.

● ●

It was kind of annoying that putting on a play took so much effort. And I am not a lazy person. It did take a TON of effort. But I didn't need to complain about much any more.

Here's what happened:

I was at Ollie's house. We were making posters for the show that we were going to hang up around town.

"Pass the purple glitter, please," I said to Ollie, who obediently handed it over. I sprinkled some on the border of glue on my neon yellow poster. "How's yours coming?" I asked Ollie. I peeked at her poster.

"Oh my gosh, Ollie, that's fantastic!" I told her enthusiastically.

"You think?" Ollie blushed and looked shy, an expression that was unusual to see on her face.

I stared at her poster again. She had only written in attention-drawing block letters at the top, COME HELP SAVE THE CALIFORNIAN REDWOODS! BUY A TICKET TO AN ORIGINAL PLAY, WRITTEN BY LOCAL GIRL ELIZA HAWTHORNE. She had drawn cute sparkly little stars in the corner, but it still looked amazing. "Definitely."

Then the phone rang. "Ollie, honey, can you pick up the phone?" Mrs. Barnes shouted from the kitchen. "My hands are covered in cookie batter!"

Ollie gave me an apologetic glance and ran out into the hallway. "Hey!" I heard her saying. "Yeah, sure. Great. Lemme go get her."

I kept on sprinkling sparkles on my posterboard, assuming Ollie was talking about her mom. I was surprised when Ollie poked her head back in the doorway and said to me, "Eliza, Jeanna is calling and she wants to talk to both of us." She lowered her voice. "She sounds really excited for some reason."

"Okay!"

"Here, you take this phone. I'll go talk on the one upstairs, so we can do three-way." Ollie thrust the phone at me and turned to walk to the stairs.

"Hello?" Jeanna's voice sounded slightly fuzzy. "Eliza? Are you there?"

"Hi!" I said. "What's new, Jeanna?"

"Lots," she said breathlessly.

"Hey, guys," Ollie interrupted. "So, Jeanna, what's the big news?"

"You have to come over. Both of you! So I can explain! It's too major to talk about on the phone."

"Ollie? Can we?" I said.

"Sure, I'll go ask my mom."

Five minutes later, Ollie and I were wheeling our bikes out of our garages and cruising down the roads, all the way to Rosebud Boulevard. Rosebud Boulevard was one of the nicest streets in all of Sparrow. If the Lemmonharts had to live in a small town, they had to live in the best part of the small town. My street (and Ollie's street also), Horace Lane, was pretty, but in a cute two-story-not-

including-the-basement-and-the-attic-which-no-
one-ever-goes-in-because-it's-a-safety-hazard-with-
all-the-nails-poking-out-of-random-places way.

Ollie used the fancy knocker on the door.
Jeanna swung the door open and beckoned us
inside. I gasped as I stepped in. The huge hallway
with the polished mahogany floor and crystal
chandelier was a little frightening to look at all at
once.

Jeanna laughed, an action I was beginning to
realize she did often. "Come on up to my room."

So, we followed Jeanna up the stairs. Jeanna's
room was large, almost as big as the family room in
my house, but it was nice and had a lived-in feeling
to it. There was a chandelier on the ceiling, like the
foyer, except this chandelier was nothing like that
ginormous looming one. This chandelier was way
less fancy and made of just glass, whereas I was
pretty sure the one in the foyer had a little bit of real
gold in it. The mini crystals dangling down from the
one in Jeanna's room were bright pink and a
butterfly shade of blue, and cast little rainbows
around the room.

Jeanna's big bed had a fuzzy comforter with
hot pink and a little bit of that soft blue making a
pattern of different sized bubbles (by bubbles, I
mean circles). She had four windows, and as a
result, her room was very sunny and she had a nice

view of the trees and mountains. Jeanna's walls were pink with lots of posters taped up of a beautiful woman who must have been her mom. I felt a little bad. It must have been sort of hard for my new friend to only get to see her mom every now and then, and have to Skype with her instead of seeing her every day. I wondered what my life would be like if my mom was a star.

But what Jeanna wanted to show us was the laptop sitting on her smooth wood desk.

That same woman who was on all of Jeanna's posters was smiling a familiar dazzling smile at us!

"Eliza and Ollie, I'd like you to meet my mom. Mom, these are my friends, Ollie and Eliza," Jeanna said.

"Ollie, we've met before! It's so nice to talk to you again. And Eliza, it's such a pleasure to meet you. Jeanna's told me all about you."

"It's nice to meet you too, Ms. Lemmonhart," I said, flashing a grin.

"Please call me Juliette, everyone does," she said.

"Uh, sure," I said, feeling slightly awkward.

"Well, Mom, tell Ollie and Eliza the news, will you? Don't keep them in suspense." Jeanna bounced up and down.

"All right, all right, but Jeanna darling, stop bouncing so much. If you break that desk chair your father will be hysterical."

Jeanna rolled her eyes. "Enough stalling, Mom!"

Her mother laughed. "Well, girls, it's sort of a long story. I guess it all began when Jeanna told me about you putting on your show so you could give the profits to Governor Corey to use to construct the buildings in a different place, and get him to change his mind about cutting down the redwoods. I understand, Eliza, that you have a personal connection to these redwoods?"

"Yes, Ms. Lemmonhart. I used to live in San Francisco, so I was nearby. We went to different parks a lot." Saying the words *San Francisco* still brought a pang to my chest, but not as big a pang as before.

"Did you know that when I was a kid, I lived in San Francisco?"

"You're kidding!" I gasped.

"No, and I loved going out to walk through the trees." Juliette Lemmonhart closed her eyes and inhaled through her nose dramatically. "I loved that fresh smell, don't you love it?"

"Yes!" I replied. It was exciting that a famous movie star liked to do the same things that I did.

Ollie and Jeanna exchanged looks, like, *What the heck are they talking about?* I giggled.

"So, Mom, get to the point!" Jeanna urged.

"Okay, okay. So, you girls and your families are getting pretty stressed with all the work of making this come together, right?"

Ollie and I nodded.

"Well, how would you girls feel if I helped direct and produce your show?"

Ollie squealed. I sucked in my breath.

"That's an awesome idea!"

"That's so nice of you!"

"Oh, wow!"

"That is so cool!"

Jeanna looked so happy she could burst at our gleeful responses. "I knew you guys would like it!"

"I'll need to talk to your parents first, of course..." Ms. Lemmonhart said, and so Ollie and I gave her our phone numbers.

"Guys?" Jeanna asked.

"Uh huh?"

"Can we spell my name G-I-N-A on the program?"

Chapter Nine

Poppy and Sydney shoved banana pancakes down their little throats while Mom, Dad and I finished singing the birthday song.

They both clapped their hands and squealed. "I'm so old!" Poppy said delightedly. "Am I older than E-wiza now?"

"Not yet, munchkin. But you and your sister are five years old! That is VERY old..." Mom replied.

"Am I old enough to get a cell phone? And drive a car?" Poppy wondered.

"Am I old enough to get two more bunnies? And get that My Little Ponies set I want?" Sydney said dreamily.

"No, no, no, maybe," said Dad, laughing, while he ticked off their requests on his fingers. "Take it easy, you rascals."

Poppy and Sydney decided they were finished with the pancakes and started on huge bowls of Coco Puffs. It was a Hawthorne tradition that you could stuff your face with as much unhealthy breakfast as you wanted on your birthday. Actually, siblings were allowed to eat like pigs too on the birthday, so I helped myself to another banana pancake.

"Can we do presents now?" Sydney asked. "Oh, please, Daddy?"

"Yes, please, Daddy?" echoed Poppy.

"Oh, no! I think we forgot to get any birthday presents this year!" Dad cried.

"Ha ha ha, Daddy, good one," the twins snickered, now moving on to syrupy waffles. This was getting a bit disgusting. Mom seemed to notice too.

"Girls, Daddy will bring your presents if you finish up your yummy breakfast. Maybe we'll save some leftovers for tomorrow morning, okay?"

Poppy and Sydney pushed away their plates and tried to follow Dad to the basement. Much to their disappointment, they were forced to wait on the couch in the family room. They bounced up and down on the sofa, causing it to rock a little. Mom had to remind them not to get very wild, otherwise their presents would be going to Cow. That quieted them down, though they still both had flushed cheeks, big smiles, and sparkling eyes.

"Hi, E-wiza!" Poppy whispered loudly. "I can't wait for presents."

"Hey, Popster. I know you can't."

"You know what, E-wiza?" Sydney said softly.

"What is it?"

"It's my birthday!" Sydney exclaimed.

"I know that, you weirdo," I said, grinning, as Poppy and Sydney started to dance and jump on the couch again.

At last, Dad walked up to the twins carrying the birthday gifts. He deposited two presents wrapped in red and blue wrapping paper with hearts all over it to Poppy, and one slightly larger gift wrapped in paper with fairies flying everywhere on it to Sydney. He dropped one present in the middle of them. "This one is for you two to share," he explained.

"No fighting over it," Mom added.

Poppy shook one of her presents. "Animal, mineral, or vegetable?" she asked, which was what she had seen someone on television do.

Sydney got that My Little Ponies set she had wanted, and Poppy got two boxes of big multicolored cardboard building blocks that looked like bricks.

"Cool!" she cried. "I can build a fort with these!"

The gift that they had to share was a huge chocolate bar that said *Happy Birthday* on it. "Maybe you can share that with your awesome older sister?" I suggested hopefully.

My present to the twins was a simple gift, but they were ecstatic about it. I had offered to do their hair elaborately and paint their nails for their party, which was in the afternoon.

"When are we gonna get started?" Poppy asked.

"Well, we can do it whenever, but I thought we should maybe do it before lunch, an hour before your party."

The twins were practicing their lines for the show. (I had changed the script so that the two mysterious men were played by Poppy and Max, Ollie's brother, instead of Sydney. Max had said he wanted to be in my show, which was nice of him. I had offered Sydney that she instead play the prisoner who was actually good and kind, because I needed someone to play the prisoner. They were equal roles with about the same amount of lines.)

So, fifty-six minutes before we had to leave to go to the kiddie gymnastics center, FunGym, I invited Poppy and Sydney to my room. I had made a sign that said, *Eliza's Spa,* and had lit a wide, thick candle scented like vanilla on my desk. The lights were dim, and it gave my "spa" a professional look. Well, at least, it looked (and smelled!) professional to Poppy and Sydney, because they started oohing and ahhing as soon as they walked in.

I had put two fuzzy pillows on the floor. "Sit," I commanded. "We'll do nails first." I had lined up all my nail polish next to the pillows. Poppy picked a neon sparkly green color, and Syd chose a shimmery shade of lavender. They sighed with delight each time I stroked the polish on their nails.

Once we were done with that step of the procedure, they had to decide what hairstyle they wanted. Poppy wanted her hair swept up, movie star-style. "No, Poppy," I answered. "You're going to be running around at your party. Something a little less glamorous, okay?" In the end, Poppy chose a fishtail braid for her curls, which she thought was the second best thing after her hair piled on top of her head. Sydney had me twist her blond waves into two pigtails and then put in a few of her favorite clips.

I spun them both around so they could see their reflections in my mirror. "Do you like it?" I said, hoping they would say yes, because I didn't want to do their nails and hair all over again.

"Yes!" Sydney cried. "Yay!"

"I look so good!" Poppy yelled. They tottered away from my room, smiling, touching their hair and examining their nails.

When they got downstairs, I heard Dad say, "Wow, look how beautiful my two birthday girls look!" Then I heard Mom say, "Did you thank your sister?"

Six minutes later, a note was slipped through

my door. It read:

THAnkS E li ZA

The twins had decorated the border of the note-card with little unicorn stickers. I could hear the twins whispering in the hall, wondering if I would write back. So, I flipped the note over.

You're welcome. Happy birthday! I love you! ☺

I slid the note back under the door.

● ●

Poppy and Sydney had allowed me to invite two friends to their party. Of course, I invited Ollie. I also invited Jeanna, because I wanted to become closer friends and her mom had been so nice about our show.

Little kids were flying everywhere. There were little kids eating pretzels in the pizza room, little kids jumping on the trampoline, little kids spilling juice boxes, and little kids running on the obstacle course that had been set up. There were also little kids walking carefully on the balance beam, which had a mat under it and was very low to the ground, just in case someone fell off. In the sea of toddlers, it was hard to find *my* two friends.

Finally, I spotted them. Ollie was helping a tiny girl named June who looked really scared down from the balance beam. Jeanna was saying goodbye to her mom, who had been in town for a few days now to help direct our show. We had rehearsals with her every afternoon at three-thirty. We all sat down at the far end of the long table in the pizza room.

"Hey guys," I said.

Jeanna grabbed a large amount of chips. "Hirlg," she said distractedly, shoving the potato chips in her mouth all at once to make us laugh.

"Eeew, Jeanna," I giggled.

"You're setting a bad example for all the kids here," Ollie scolded, but it was obvious she thought it was hilarious.

Jeanna swallowed the chips. "Is it a CRIME to be a hungry person? No, I don't think so," she said, pouting theatrically.

Ollie shoved a juice box at her. "Drink this to wash down all that salt." She made a face.

"Did you bring the cake?" I asked Ollie. Mrs. Barnes had offered to bake the cake for the party.

"Yup, and she wrote *Happy Birthday, Poppy and Sydney* on the top in different colored icing, with little yellow candy stars all over the cake. Also, she put green and pink colored sugar on the top and cookie crumbles too, and the inside is a vanilla and chocolate swirly patterned thing, with some strawberry ice cream."

Jeanna licked her lips. "I daresay, that sounds soooo good," and Ollie and I start to make fun of her for saying "daresay."

All the children fill in to eat their lunch. Pizza slices on plates with princesses on them get passed around. The three of us and the grown-ups make sure everybody has a juice box and a blue napkin.

Once Poppy and Sydney's friends were all set, we sat back down. "So we're still having rehearsal today?" I asked, slurping on an apple juice box. Our show was actually now going to be located at Jeanna's backyard instead of mine, because, well... I didn't really know, but it probably had something to do with the size of her yard, and Juliette Lemmonhart directing the show.

"Yes," Jeanna replied, "but because of the twins' party, it's going to be at four. Is that okay?"

"It's okay by me," Ollie said. "Max, I guess, will be fine with it too."

"It's okay with me too, but we might be a little late because Poppy and Sydney are going to be opening their presents at home and stuff," I said.

Around two hours later, the kids started to pick

up their goodie-bags and leave. Poppy and Sydney said goodbye to everyone at the door. All the children they had invited had gone to their two-week day camp. They said "see you at school," because Sparrow was such a small town that the girls and boys who were at the party would all be in Poppy and Sydney's class this autumn.

After everybody had gone except for the twins, Ollie, Jeanna, my parents, Ollie's mom, and me, we all headed out too. Jeanna was going home with Ollie's family.

After the twins had opened all the presents - plenty of arts-and-crafts, dolls, toys, games, and books - we all walked to Jeanna's house.

I held the twins' hands and we walked right into Jeanna's backyard, which was what Jeanna's mom told us we should always do for rehearsals. Raspberry, Jeanna's little dog, yipped excitedly at us and went over to lick Poppy and Sydney. They immediately bent over and scratched Raspberry's fur, and Poppy squeaked, "Hi, Razzy!"

The Lemmonharts' backyard was already almost set up for the show, which was in three days. There was a large rental stage sitting in a perfect place, with a big black wall sort of thing in the back for backstage. The stage was right in front of fifteen rows of matching white folding chairs. There were two long white tables in the back.

The tickets to my show were almost sold out, and I couldn't believe it. I didn't know that so many people felt so strongly about helping the redwoods. But then again, it probably helped that famous Juliette Lemmonhart was directing it and would be making an appearance at the beginning, reading aloud a speech I had written all about the redwoods. Ms. Lemmonhart had even ordered a hundred nice brochures with plenty of facts about northern Californian nature and beautiful pictures. After the show, we were going to sell refreshments to the audience (supplied by the Sweet Apron, of course!).

Ms. Lemmonhart was talking in the corner of the backyard, her brow furrowed, to our costume designer, Gabrielle de la Dassault. Gabrielle had measured us yesterday.

Ms. Lemmonhart was saying "...yes, yes, we need Eliza and Ollie in old-fashioned tunic-dresses with three-quarter sleeves, with leggings and leather girls' boots. A violet dress with a high waist and black leggings for Eliza, a sky blue dress with a high waist with...actually, maybe with butterfly sleeves for Ollie and black leggings too. It should transform, in a quick change during a black-out, into the same thing, basically, but more ragged and dirty-looking. Uh huh, you've got it. Jeanna will need a long, black velvet dress with a high collar and an Empire waist, and a large steel crown with black stones… yes, yes, you know the type. It should have an evil sort of feeling to it. Go crazy, just make these three costumes fabulous with magnificent touches from your imagination like you always do. The men, the mysterious men, they'll need nothing too extravagant. Just black-hooded cloaks and silver-colored masks and black pants and tunics will be fine. The other captive, the prisoner, should just wear a tattered gown, I guess, but it needs to be easy to move in for little Sydney…"

"Oui, do you want the gown to be colorful or drab-colored?" Gabrielle had a thick French accent, so when she said "colored" it sounded like "colort."

While Gabrielle and Ms. Lemmonhart continued their conversation, I headed over to where Ollie and Jeanna were sitting with a bowl of Goldfish crackers in between them. "I just heard all about our costumes!" I said.

Ollie popped a Goldfish in her mouth and motioned for me to sit next to her. "Yeah?" she said. "What are they like?

I rushed into happy detail about the tunic-dresses and furry boots, and Jeanna's sophisticated dress with the big glamorous crown.

"Cool!" Jeanna exclaimed. "I've always wanted to wear an evil queen's crown."

"Yeah, it must have been your life-long passion and desire," Ollie remarked dryly, and we laughed.

We wandered over to the entrance of the backyard to gaze at the beautiful welcome and admissions sign Ollie had made. WELCOME, the sign read. Ollie had used her fanciest writing. PLEASE GO TO THE STAND TO YOUR LEFT SO WE CAN CHECK YOUR TICKET/S. ENJOY THE SHOW, AND THANK YOU FOR SUPPORTING THE REDWOODS. My mom would be at the admissions desk.

"It's so pretty," I sighed. "Ollie, you really *are* an amazing artist."

Ollie grinned modestly. "Shut up, Eliza."

There was a joyful little bark. Max had thrown a stick across the lawn and Raspberry had raced over to retrieve it.

"Okay, everyone!" shouted Ms. Lemmonhart, some honey-colored hair falling out of her casual ponytail. "Let's get started."

We all crowd around her. She shoos Raspberry away. "Okay, girls - and guy," Ms. Lemmonhart added, giving a thumbs-up to Max. "Our show is in three days. Is anyone nervous?" Jeanna put her hand up in the air. So did Ollie and Max. The twins just nodded. I glanced around, then put my hand up too.

"That's good!" Ms. Lemmonhart smiled warmly.

"Uh, why is it *good*?" Max blurted.

"Good question. It's good to be nervous because it shows you really care about the production," Ms. Lemmonhart said, and Jeanna nodded.

"Oh." Max shoved his hands in his pockets, no doubt trying to find his sound machine tucked in there. Sure enough, after a minute, I heard a tiny noise that sounded suspiciously like *wheeeeeeeeeeeeooooshhh - SPLAT!*

We three older girls grinned.

"Anyway, shall we start the rehearsal?" Juliette asked. When we nodded, she continued, "Okay, let's start it from Scene Nine. It needs some last minute touch-ups…"

We all took our places on the rental stage.

"Dawn?" I called out.

"Azalea?" Ollie called back. "Where are you?"

"I'm right here… when I managed to get out the door I walked into another cell…there's another prisoner here in this wretched tower!" I said dramatically.

Ollie went through the door we had on the stage. It was to be rolled on during the captivity scenes, and off when they weren't taking place. She joined Sydney and me.

The prisoner/Sydney explained to Dawn/Ollie what she had explained to Azalea/me.

"I," she said, "was brought here twenty years ago, by some men in black hoods. I couldn't see their faces. They were masked."

"So were we!" Ollie cried, motioning at me. *She's a really good actress,* I thought.

Before she said her line, Sydney started to crack her knuckles, which was one of her bad habits.

"Cut!" Ms. Lemmonhart announced. "Sydney, honey, I know it's hard, but when we perform, let's try not to crack our knuckles. Your character is weakened, and scared of these mean men. She is very, very sad that she has been locked up for so long. Okay? Come on, honey, you can do this!" Ms. Lemmonhart gave her a thumbs-up. "Make your face look like you are very tired, hungry, and sad, okee dokee?" She demonstrated. "Like this."

Sydney did her tired, hungry, sad face, and Juliette smiled. "Good."

We continued. "They said I had insulted the queen, and I said to them, 'your queen is evil and I will never go to her side…you can take me away. I never will go to her side, never, never…'" Sydney looked up at us from the floor with huge eyes. "I am now old, and weak. I know a way out, but am too feeble to use it. I am dying…I am feeble, I…?" Sydney paused, forgetting the rest of her line.

Ms. Lemmonhart called out, "And I am nearing death."

"And I am nearing death," Sydney repeated, finishing her line.

I gasped. "That's horrible. What is your name?"

"I do not remember my name, though I wish I did… Why are you two young girls here?"

"I bet it was our fathers, Azalea." Ollie was projecting, but she made her voice sound soft in a way.

I bowed my head, and then explained to Sydney's character how our fathers were dead now, but they were the queen's two brothers. Azalea and Dawn were cousins along with being friends. They had decided they would rather be good and kind and fight her than be cruel and evil and join her.

"I am dying," Sydney said simply. "If I tell you the way out of this tower, will you go and get revenge on the queen for me?"

Ollie nodded. "Yes, of course we will!" I replied.

And our rehearsal went on and on, until Scene Nine was over. Jeanna, Poppy, and Max started applauding from where they were sitting, watching us.

"That was good, Eliza, Ollie, and Sydney. Excellent work. I can tell you've been practicing." Ms. Lemmonhart said, right after her husband, Jeanna's dad, Aaron Sherman (Jeanna had obviously taken her mother's last name), walked into the yard. He told us he'd been listening in his study and that it sounded stupendous. My ears glowed red with pride.

Governor Corey was going DOWN. My play was going to be a huge success!

Chapter Ten

I have so many butterflies in my stomach!"
Ollie shrieked quietly.

I smoothed down my long French braid and
straightened my purple tunic-dress. I peeked out
from the black curtain and wall that was backstage.
There were so many people sitting out there,
chatting happily or leafing through redwood books,
waiting for the show to begin. My brain spun.
Would all these people buying ten-dollar tickets to
my show be enough to convince the governor to
leave the redwoods alone? There were about a
hundred and twenty-five people here so far. *Wow,
that's a LOT*.

"Me too," I admitted. "This is nuts."

Jeanna grinned. "I, however, am confident that
long black dresses with huge tall collars and silver
crowns will instantly become the new fad!" Jeanna
touched her hair, which was swept up with lots of
hairspray and some strands straggling down. Ollie's
hair was just loose, but our hair stylist had twisted a
little piece of her hair and then clipped it back with
a black shiny barrette. It looked really pretty.

"I just hope this will produce enough money to

get the governor to change his mind," I said anxiously.

"Don't worry, Eliza! We can do this!" Jeanna said enthusiastically.

"Yeah, if after we get to Sacramento and talk to him he still won't change his idiotic mind, he'll have ME to answer to!" Ollie growled. I laughed nervously.

I drifted off to wish good luck to my twin sisters. Oh, wait. Hadn't Jeanna said something about how it's actually *bad* luck to wish an actor good luck before a production? She had said, "Instead, you say, 'break a leg.'" Jeanna was experienced at acting, so I decided I would take her word for it. Still a touch confused, I said, "Well, break a leg! You guys are gonna be awesome, and you both look so pretty."

"Why are we going to break our legs?!" asked Poppy frantically. Sydney was cracking her knuckles, looking worried.

"Don't worry, Pop, it's just an expression that means you're going to do super great!" I reassured her. Both twins let out sighs of relief.

"Break a leg, too, E-wiza," Sydney said shyly, hugging me.

"Yes, you will do super great too!" Poppy added, giving me another hug.

I moved on to say break a leg to Max, and then

I found my parents waiting for me.

"You're going to do great, Eliza," Dad said, squeezing my hand.

"We are so proud of you, honey," said Mom.

"Those redwoods are definitely going to be safe," Dad said.

"Break a leg, Eliza!" And with one last hug, they both were gone.

The show was about to begin. I felt my stomach lurch as I joined Ollie and Jeanna.

"I feel like I'm gonna throw up," I said quietly.

"So do I," Ollie groaned.

"Third the motion!" Jeanna whispered. "But that is a normal part of acting, my mom told me."

We all listened silently while Juliette Lemmonhart walked onstage and the audience hushed immediately.

"Welcome," she said graciously. "We are so glad you're here. For those of you who don't know me -" Ollie gave a little snort. Practically everybody in the world knew who Juliette Lemmonhart was, but it was still nice for her to say that.

" - I am Juliette Lemmonhart."

"Yeah, Juli!" someone in the audience cheered. I peeked out of the curtain and saw Ms. Lemmonhart's red-lipstick mouth curve into a big smile.

"However, we are all here to see an amazing

production not because of me," she continued.

She started the little speech. "When eleven-year-old aspiring playwright Eliza Hawthorne discovered she would be moving to Sparrow, our small town in the Berkshires, all the way from San Francisco, California, she knew she would miss something more than anything back in California. Eliza grew up walking through the Northern Californian redwood trees, and she would miss them dearly. However, she has grown to love Sparrow like everyone else who steps foot in our charming town, and made friends. She realized that the redwoods would always be there, and she would be able to visit every now and then.

"Until, one day, Eliza got a shocking letter from a friend back in San Francisco. Governor Corey of California is clearing out a park of redwoods outside the city in order to build more apartment buildings, stores, and hotels so that the state can be more successful in collecting taxes." I could hear the disapproval in Ms. Lemmonhart's voice.

"Meanwhile, Eliza had just finished up the first play she had written in Sparrow, an adventurous tale of two girls and an evil queen. With the help of her two friends, Ollie Barnes and Jeanna Lemmonhart, she made up her mind to perform her show in front of an audience and sell tickets. Then the day after the play, the three would fly to Sacramento and give Governor Corey the proceeds from the show, so he could use the money to construct buildings somewhere else.

"So, thank you all for coming to *Azalea and Dawn's Adventure*. The redwoods thank you, too!" Ms. Lemmonhart finished. People laughed and applauded.

The spotlight glaring on the stage went out. I swallowed and took my place with Ollie on the stage. I suddenly was hot and sweaty in my long boots. I felt frozen, and wondered if I would unfreeze before the lights shone on the stage again.

Then the spotlight came on. I blinked. *Please don't let this be a failure, please don't let this be a failure, please don't let this be a failure, PLEASE don't let this be a failure*, I repeated in my head.

In that moment, I quickly glanced at the audience. They were all smiling at me, waiting for the show to start. They were *smiling*. That meant they had hope. So would I, I decided.

I inhaled slowly, and I looked at Ollie to tell her we could start. Ollie caught my eye, then grinned at me. I grinned back. We linked arms and sat down together on a fake-marble bench on the stage. We mimed talking happily, our lips moving, but no sound coming out. The screen behind us was showing a pleasant grassy field that looked like the "backyard" of a castle. The sky on the screen kept getting darker and darker, as the day went on. Ollie and I mimed girls playing together through the day. Ollie moved her mouth, talking silently, still grinning and mime-laughing, hopping up on the bench occasionally and pretending to make a speech. I did a cartwheel, then dusted off my hands, still grinning. Ollie clapped with no noise.

At last, the sky on the screen was a deep indigo. I checked my watch and made obvious motions with my hands: Azalea and Dawn should go back home, their mothers would be getting worried. I had added in this relaxed, soothing part of Scene One right before I had finished writing the play. This little, two-minute part was meant to show how carefree the two friends had been before they embarked on their long journey.

Right as Ollie and I were about to exit the stage entirely, Poppy and Max came on, right in front of us. They started walking toward us. Ollie and I were backing away. They ran at us and chained us together.

Ollie and I screamed. The audience startled a little. "You stop that!" I yelled.

"Unchain my hands right now!" Ollie exclaimed.

And the show went on and on. In the few scenes I wasn't in, I watched the audience's expressions worriedly from a narrow space in between the curtains.

What would happen if this didn't work? If the governor didn't change his mind? Negative thoughts whizzed through my head. Governor Corey was obviously a ridiculously stubborn man when he got an idea. What if an eleven-year-old (twelve in October!) girl wasn't enough to convince him to leave the trees alone?

I was a nature-lover; the governor was not. I was a tree-hugger; the governor was not. I was a playwright; the governor was not. I thought the redwoods should be left alone; the governor did not. Would we see eye to eye about *anything*?

I heard Jeanna's voice rise as she acted out a scene with Poppy and Max. "NO! It is essential, you must do as I tell you, otherwise I will fail!" She let out a wail of rage. "Why must you be so ignorant?" Jeanna stomped off the stage. As she joined me behind the curtain on the right side, I gave her a big thumbs-up. "Thanks," Jeanna mouthed. She smiled. I went back on the stage to perform my scene.

I cringed as I tripped on the flat platform. How clumsy! But then I remembered a quote Ollie had showed me. *It takes skill to trip over a flat surface.* Ollie was probably remembering too, because we caught each other's eyes as we entered from different sides of the stage. I heard a little laughter from the audience. Happy laughter, not making-fun-of-you laughter. *Good.* I held my head higher.

And still, the show kept on going. And then we were on THE. LAST. SCENE. Oh my gosh, oh my gosh, oh my gosh!

"You won't be capturing and killing off anyone anymore," Dawn/Ollie said evenly.

"Yes. You see, Dawn and I think it's time for somebody else to be in charge. We were thinking of our friend back in the tower. We'd take her to the doctor and get her healed before she gets the job, though. Dawn?" Azalea/I looked Dawn/Ollie in the eye.

"No!" Evil Queen/Jeanna cried. "You two will be sorry you ever dared -"

"Oh, shut up," Ollie said in a bored way. "For once."

"How do you think we should get rid of her?" I asked her.

"Oh…the Wicked-Witch-Way!" Ollie said.

"No! Not the Wic -" Jeanna started.

"Yeah, good idea." I cut her off. This was the part where Poppy was supposed to come onstage holding out a big bucket of water, which Ollie and I would take. Then, we would pour it on Jeanna's head, and she would "melt" into her long black dress. The "melt" technique was a little tricky, but

Ms. Lemmonhart managed to teach her daughter how to do it.

But Poppy didn't come.

And she still wasn't here.

The awkwardness of me just standing there seemed to last an eternity. I could feel the heat rising in my cheeks. I knew I looked like an idiot. Where was Poppy? Where was Poppy?

I caught Ollie's eye, and from her reaction I realized I also looked panicked.

Get a grip, Eliza Brooke Hawthorne, I told myself. "Does anyone have a bucket of water here?" I ad-libbed (which means making something up on the spot). I wanted Poppy to hear me. I waited a moment. No such luck. All right, then. It was time for some big-time improvising.

I sighed impatiently. "Wow, Ms. Evil Queen. Your haunted castle has *really* slow service." The audience laughed. Ollie and Jeanna watched me, bewildered. I scanned the crowd, hoping desperately my idea would work.

I took a huge breath and stepped off the stage. A person in the audience gasped. I walked over to a cute little boy with blond hair in the front row of the audience who was clutching a water bottle patterned with multicolored cars and trucks.

"Hi!" I said loudly to the small boy, who looked to be around the age of two. I pointed to his water bottle. "Could I use that for a sec? I promise I'll return it after." The little boy stared up at me, and, looking extremely confused, but smiling a wide toddler grin, held out his water bottle. I took it. The audience started roaring with laughter. They were so loud, I thought my eardrums might burst.

I stepped back onto the stage and quickly glanced at Ollie and Jeanna's faces, trying to see if they understood. They did. Relief flooded through my body.

"Ooh, nice, Azalea," Ollie said, smiling.

"Will you help with the honors?" I said to her.

"But of course," said Ollie, and together we dumped the contents of the bottle on Jeanna's head. Wailing and moaning dramatically, Jeanna melted into her dress, and finally, all the audience could see of her was a black velvet mess on the floor of the stage. The audience started to roar with that crazy laughter again, and they also started to clap.

"Wait!" I yelled over the very loud applause. "WAIT!"

Everyone went quiet. "Um -" I hopped off the stage once more. I approached the little kid who had lent me his water bottle. I kneeled down so I could be at his eye level and handed him his water bottle. "What's your name?" I said kindly.

The boy gave me a grin, his insanely huge eyes sparkling with mischief. "Tobby! Tobby!" he hollered, jumping out of his chair and doing a small, weird dance for the audience, who sighed in delight over this cute little kid.

"Um, what's his name?" I turned to the woman next to him who looked like his mom.

"Tommy," the lady replied.

"Well, Tommy," I said, and he stopped dancing and looked at me. "Tommy, I'd like to thank you. The kingdom owes you one." He squealed happily, and everybody started to clap and chuckle again. I gave Tommy a hug, and then walked back onstage.

The twins and Max bowed first, all together. Jeanna bowed by herself. Then Ollie bowed.

So I took a bow. The applause was deafening.

Chapter Eleven

Governor Corey's leering face cackled at me. "You," he smiled evilly, "will never, never save the redwoods. Never! NEVER! MWA HA HA -"

"Eliza! Wake up, Eliza!" I opened my eyes and Ollie's face swam into view.

"Are you okay?" asked Jeanna, who was perched precariously on the edge of my bed. "You were screaming things like, 'no, please,' and, 'no…NO!' Did you have a bad dream?"

I looked around the room. It did not look like my room in Sparrow. And then I remembered: Ollie, Jeanna, and I were in our suite at L'Orre hotel in Sacramento, California. I could hear Ms. Lemmonhart in the connected suite blow-drying her hair.

I shuddered. "Yes. Governor Corey was haunting my dreams all night."

Ollie made a sympathetic face. "It's okay."

"Eliza, you need to get out of bed. Mom said that you're expected at the Capitol at eleven o'clock." Jeanna scolded.

I glanced over at the clock next to my bed. The clock claimed it was ten-thirty. Oh no!

I threw off my covers. "This is what Juliette wants you to wear," Ollie said, tossing me a soft, pretty blouse that was pale yellow. "She says to wear it with your gray jeans that you packed, and your black ballet flats. Oh, and don't forget this!" A headband with a pastel yellow and light gray pattern hit me on my left ear.

"Why so fancy?" I mumbled, dragging myself to my candy-red suitcase to get my gray skinny jeans and black flats.

"We're all fancy, Eliza, not just you," Jeanna insisted. She was wearing a gray skirt and a frilly bright bubble-gum colored top, I noticed. Ollie was wearing delicate silver sandals and a fancy dark blue shirt that had thin black stripes on it.

I sighed and put on the blouse. I scrambled to the bathroom mirror to brush my long hair, and after that, neatly put on the headband. Jeanna thrust at me a blueberry muffin that she had bought in the restaurant downstairs last night. After eating it in three bites, I brushed my teeth quickly.

Ms. Lemmonhart entered into our room. "Good morning, Eliza, thank you for getting ready so quickly. There will be a car picking us up in five minutes. Come on, girls, let's go!"

I stared at Ms. Lemmonhart's outfit. Her red and black skirt, white shirt and black high heels made her look like…well, look like a movie star.

We all piled into the elevator, and I pressed the button for the lobby. While Ollie and Jeanna struck up a conversation together about how exciting it was to be in California, and what they wanted to see once we'd saved the redwoods, I gazed at the floor, distracted. I tapped my shoes on the floor.

I chewed on my lower lip, extremely nervous and jittery. I recited my greeting to the governor in my head. *Hello, Governor Corey. My name is -*

"Eliza!" Jeanna called. "We're getting off the elevator, Eliza."

Five minutes later, the four of us sat down in a black shiny stretch limo.

"Where d'you want to go to?" the gruff chauffeur asked, fiddling with the GPS.

"The Capitol," Ms. Lemmonhart replied. The chauffeur looked back at her and gasped.

"Are you Juliette Lemmonhart?" the driver choked out.

Jeanna, Ollie, and I all let out nervous, tight laughs. Ms. Lemmonhart told him she was. But after that, no one spoke for a while.

The little TV in the limo was on the news station. "Governor Corey is cutting down a large reservation of redwoods," the man on the news was saying. "Hundreds of people are protesting outside of the Capitol Building in Sacramento, but apparently nothing will change the governor's mi-"

I stared at the miniature screen with a stony expression, willing it in my head to shut up. Ms. Lemmonhart noticed.

"So, girls," she said fake-brightly, "I think we'll be there in a minute or two."

And abruptly, we were.

I found myself standing in front of a huge off-white building. There were pillars and a big dome. I felt very small. I wondered if that was where the governor worked. A short distance away, a protesting crowd kept yelling at the building, "SAVE THE REDWOODS!" and "LET THE TREES BE!" and "WE WANT THE REDWOODS TO STAY!"

Ollie walked up to me. "You'll do so well," she said softly.

Those words of encouragement almost brought tears to my eyes.

"Thanks," I whispered to my first friend in Sparrow.

Jeanna came over, and for once she didn't know what to say. "I…you're going to do it, Eliza. I can tell." I tried to swallow the huge softball-sized lump in my throat. Jeanna and Ollie were such good friends. They both held onto one of my hands, and we followed Ms. Lemmonhart into the Capitol, the three of us linked together.

I could hardly breathe. I kept on feeling my

heart abruptly beat. I looked around while Ms. Lemmonhart talked to a crisp-looking lady at the front desk. And all the while, I still held onto Ollie and Jeanna's hands.

"Oh, yes, I think I remember you calling," said the woman to Ms. Lemmonhart. "Get the girls, and you'll go on up to his office. There's a little private seating area outside the office so you, Miss Jeanna and Miss Ollie can sit while Miss Eliza discusses her problem with the governor. Come."

Jeanna, Ollie, and I scurried over. I shivered. The building was cold and I was wearing a short-sleeved blouse. The woman led us to the elevator and told Ms. Lemmonhart the floor and number of the governor's office. "Good luck," the lady said, and as the door of the elevator slid shut, she winked at me. That wink made me stand a little taller.

We arrived at the floor where the governor worked. We walked down a long hall and at last, approached the door of the governor's office. My heart thumped wildly.

Ms. Lemmonhart squeezed my shoulders. "Knock," she whispered. I knocked.

The door swung open and a man in a gray pinstriped suit and tie came into view. He gave me a really obvious fake smile. "Is this the little girl who sent me two dozen letters begging me not to cut down the trees?"

I blushed, but I kept glaring at him. "Hello, Governor Corey."

"We'll be out here, Eliza," said Ms. Lemmonhart. Ollie and Jeanna nodded. With one last desperate look over my shoulder at them, they were gone.

"Can I come in?" I asked. I was still standing in the hall.

"I suppose," the governor replied briskly, looking at his watch. I stepped into his office and sat down in a chair across from his desk. He sat down at the desk.

"My name is Eliza Hawthorne. And to set the record straight, I'm almost twelve."

"How lovely for you!" Governor Corey said, a real smirk on his face this time. "Unfortunately for you, Eliza Hawthorne, it's going to take more than an almost-twelve-year-old girl to change my mind."

"Huh. Really," I said breezily.

The governor arched an eyebrow. "Look, Elise... "

"It's Eliza," I corrected him.

"Well, *Eliza*," the governor continued, "I really don't have time for this nonsense. I've hardly been able to work lately because of those ridiculous protestors."

I realized I could hear the crowd of people shrieking louder than before up in the governor's office.

"You do know that they're mad at you for a reason?" I said coldly.

"I don't want to hear more about those redwoods!" Governor Corcy snapped, standing up. "You have no idea what I'm going through! You're just another naive person who has absolutely no idea what the real issues are, aren't you!"

"You..." I shut my mouth. What I had been about to say was, *You're describing yourself, Governor,* but letting my temper get a hold of me wouldn't solve my problem.

"I'm right! You're wrong! The protestors are wrong! The irksome press is wrong! The redwoods must go!" the governor bellowed, breathing very fast.

"Please listen," I said forcefully, "or we'll never get anything achieved here."

"Who are you to order me around?" Governor Corey demanded, but he sat down anyway. "You don't understand! California needs to be more successful in our buildings up north. Less nature, more construction, more buildings, more taxes, Elizabeth."

"It's *Eliza*!" Why couldn't this guy *listen*? I took a deep breath. "Governor Corey." I started over. "*You* don't understand. The redwood parks in California mean a lot to me. I grew up walking through them, recording facts about them, doing projects on them, and just letting myself think as I sat under them. The redwoods mean a lot to a bunch of other people, too." I gestured toward the protestors outside the window. "Or can't you tell?"

"I don't see what -"

"As I told you in one of my" I made quotation marks with my fingers "*two dozen* letters, I wrote a play and performed it with my friends in front of the whole town. We raised five thousand dollars through ticket sales."

Governor Corey's mouth dropped open.

"That's right. And my plan was that I'd give you the five thousand dollars to help pay for putting the buildings somewhere else, and leaving the redwoods alone."

"It would be so humiliating…so embarrassing…" the governor muttered.

Something inside me snapped completely. "So what? You set yourself up for the humiliation by hatching that horrible plan to chop down a forest of redwoods! If only you hadn't started that in the first place, you wouldn't be sitting here, going through all this right now!" I bit my tongue. How would the governor react to my outburst?

To my huge surprise, he shrunk down in his seat. "You're the only one who came with a check. Even though lots of people have come to me with the same demand," he said, sounding very weak and reluctant.

I closed my eyes. Would he agree?

"All right. Let's just be done with this," he managed. "I can't fight against all these people any longer. It will hurt my plans for reelection."

Still shocked, I handed him the check. "Goodbye, Governor Corey."

I shut the door firmly behind me.

When I got into the hallway, I started running towards Ollie, Jeanna and Ms. Lemmonhart.

I hurled myself at my friends and started to sob.

Ollie, Jeanna, and Ms. Lemmonhart understood at once that I was crying of happiness. And then Ms. Lemmonhart started crying. And Jeanna. And Ollie.

I smiled through my tears.

I had saved the redwoods.

Epilogue

I wake up before the alarm clock goes off.

I throw off my covers and start to get ready. After all, I need to be quick. Ollie Barnes and Jeanna Lemmonhart are picking me up in forty-five minutes.

As I brush my teeth, I wonder how my first day at Sparrow Middle will be. I can't help but worry - it's my first day of sixth grade, and my first day at my new school. Will people like me? Will I like them? However, there are also way more positive thoughts running through my brain. I haven't been this excited for school since I was five.

I wander into my sister's room and give Cow a good-morning stroke. I love that crazy rabbit.

I walk down the flight of stairs. Mom, Dad, Poppy, and Sydney are all at the kitchen table, eating breakfast. Poppy and Sydney are chattering away together, incredibly hyper. For a split second I wonder if Mom let them drink some of her coffee. Then I realize that today is their first day of kindergarten.

"ELIZA!" they screech when they see me. They've been able to pronounce their L's even better for the past week or so.

"Goodness, girls! I'm sure you just woke up the whole neighborhood!" Mom chides, but she's holding back a smile.

I sit down at the table and pour myself a bowl of Cheerios. I scoop up a spoonful and crunch down on it in my mouth. "Let me guess - you guys are excited for the first day of school?"

"Good morning, Eliza," my dad says, sipping his tea and reading the newspaper.

"Hi, Dad." I grin.

The doorbell rings just as Poppy, Sydney, and I are finishing up breakfast.

"Bye, Mom," I say, giving her a hug. "Bye, Dad," I say, giving him a hug. "C'mon, Poppy and Sydney."

I swing open the front door. Ollie and Jeanna are waiting there for me. As soon as Poppy and Sydney see Max, they run ahead with him.

Ollie, Jeanna, and I walk in thoughtful silence. As we walk, I have a flashback of the first time the doorbell rang.

It was Ollie, welcoming us to town. I had been unfriendly and cold, wishing I were back in San Francisco. I didn't realize I could love both San Francisco and Sparrow. I thought I had to choose one. Ollie was my first true friend here.

I have another flashback, of when I first met Jeanna this time. I had also snubbed her, thinking her impolite and boastful. I didn't look deep enough to see what a wonderful person she is. I think back to how she generous she was and how she helped us enormously with my play, including getting her mom involved.

And the time when Ollie and I made tie-dyed mud pies at the Lake! When Jeanna helped out at my sister's birthday party! When the three of us put on a show together.

"I had a great summer," I think aloud.

"Me too," Ollie agrees.

"Don't forget me!" Jeanna adds.

I realize with a start that we're arriving at Sparrow Middle. We're approaching the main doors of the school. I take a deep breath. I look over to my two friends standing beside me, and I suddenly know for sure that they will stay by my side.

Am I ready for this?

I smile.

I am.

And my heart soars with joy.

About the Author

Abby Richmond is in sixth grade and lives in the Boston area. She loves to act, sing, play piano, play soccer, and especially loves to read and write. Abby's favorite authors are J.K. Rowling, Louisa May Alcott, Heather Vogel Frederick and Wendy Mass. The nature theme of *Starring Eliza* was inspired by a day that Abby spent hiking in Muir Woods outside San Francisco. Abby's first book was *Very Berry*, which raised over $1,600 for the organization Reading is Fundamental (RIF). More information about *Starring Eliza* and *Very Berry* can be found at www.abbyrichmondbooks.com.

21875552R00070

Made in the USA
Charleston, SC
05 September 2013